SECRETS
& RUIN

MONICA AGENO

SECRETS & RUIN

Copyright © <2021> <Monica Ageno>

All rights reserved.

ISBN: 978-0-6452878-8-2
Published by Kingdom Books.

This is a work of fiction. Names, places, characters and incidents are the product of the author's imagination and are fictitious. Any resemblance to actual persons, living or dead, events or establishments is solely coincidental.

A Warning From Guma

Here is the deal, I am not a hero, I am not even the good guy
in this story.
I am practical. If someone stands in my way, I remove them.
If something amuses me, I play with it. I am the assumed and
feared witch doctor of this dreadfully backward village, where
this unfortunate story occurs.
This story contains violence, murder and assault of the sexual
nature. This world is a dark, savage place. A place where women
are cruel and men are spineless bastards at best and depraved
monsters at worst. Brace yourself! Fate does tinker with surprises,
so let's dance shall we?

1

Alice Odyek had five sons. Guma was one of them. He was an artist. The first time Winyo saw him, he was drawing. That was weeks ago.

Today he was drawing again. From behind the long blades of grass and cruel looking shrubs, Winyo and her best friend Acholla spied on him. It was not an ideal hiding place. The afternoon rain had soaked the ground like water to a sponge; the swaying blades of grass gaily whipping in the air, sprayed cold droplets of water and the weathered grass on the ground was soggy and equally unyielding. No one in their right mind would take an afternoon to lounge on it. Guma wasn't exactly what everyone called normal.

Come to think of it, all the things that happened to Winyo started just around that time. The time when the Odyek family returned, like flocks of bats from a night trip.

Naturally Winyo wouldn't have dared venture into the dark bushes to spy on him. The overly inquisitive Acholla, on the other hand, showed no such restraint. Upon sighting his bright blue shirt against the green of the vegetation, Acholla had made it her mission to see what he was up to. She practically dragged Winyo into the bush with her.

Of course, the stories were many; *'he goes to the bush to plot theft.'* Consequently, stories of properties disappearing from houses and animals being stolen began to emerge. Some said he went to the bushes to make offerings of animal sacrifices to the gods. The gossip started along the lines of *'what does he go to draw?'* *'He is always drawing,'* then, *'could it be more than just drawing? Could he be up to something?'*

Either way, in Winyo's village, Pomolo, the stories surrounding the Odyek family were numerous. The small northern Ugandan village was a very long distance from Kitgum town. The town where the Odyek family was rumoured to have been living, ever since they had left Pomolo, several years back.

Their sudden appearance had come as a surprise to the entire village. Winyo could not tell whether it was necessarily an unpleasant surprise. For, although the stories were terrible, the village was more abuzz than ever, and gossip was passed around with careless abundance like the local brew at a drink fest.

It was said that Alice Odyek was a witch doctor who had been responsible for the death of some children in the village and for a number of atrocities that had befallen some of the villagers. Her husband Okeny Odyek had no pleasant stories about him either. He was a businessman who had been known for cheating, and on numerous occasions had been accused of looting and several questionable business activities.

Years back, the stories about them had grown so much, causing such uproar in the village to near explosion. That was when they had been forced to move to Kitgum town. However, the tales had lingered on like the stench of stale milk despite the family's absence from the village. That was how Winyo knew of them even before she had met them.

Winyo was sure that she had heard no mention of them during her times in Kitgum town. She went to school there, to the small boarding school called Atanga Girls. She had been lucky. Her father had been reluctant to pay her fees for secondary education, but she had aced her primary leaving exams and had qualified for a government sponsorship.

She loved Kitgum town. It was a pleasant town. It was not a very big town, but anyone would fit in and anyone could be whatever they wanted to be. Everyone seemed accepting of the other. In Kitgum town, no one knew of the Odyek family, like they did in her village.

In her village, the Odyek house was miles away from the rest of the other houses. No one had attempted to build near it despite their absence. Perhaps, it was the house that had captured their essence and remained like an ugly scar in the village. Every stranger that travelled the path beside the house got to hear about the Odyek family. The stories about this cursed family lingered on with the intensity of the December heat wave, yet maintaining the endless dreamy spice of folklore.

It was an iron roofed house, one of the few such houses in the village. It was a big house. It stood alone like the last ripe mango at the end of a dry season but possessing the eerie feeling of a haunted house.

Only the ever-carefree grass dared wander around the cursed compound, dancing on the walls in blissful whispers and deliberately choreographed patterns that only nature could provide.

It was a farmer returning late from the fields who had witnessed the arrival of the Odyek family. Within no time, the news had spread around the village like the plague. People were terrified at first.

Soon, it was known that Okeny Odyek had passed away and that had been the reason for the family's appearance in the village. His wife had come to bring his body home for burial. No one attended the burial. Formally, that is. The villagers stood far away from the burial scene like ants scattered by drops of water. Their fear and contempt were as subtle as a trumpet blast.

Only a few grave diggers had lingered close by, but they were only waiting for the payment of their services.

Naturally, one would expect the Odyeks to leave Pomolo after the burial, right? But wonder of wonders, they had stayed.

A few days back when Winyo was delivering flour to one of the homes past the Odyek residence, she had noticed that the place was shuddering with activities. The Odyek boys were on the roof, repairing the iron sheets to their house while some had white paint for the walls.

The bushes inside the compound had been cleared away. The huge white stones paving the way to the house were scrubbed till they were shining once more and were well aligned into a welcoming pattern. Not that anyone would come by. This confirmed that for some reason known only to them, they were going to stay on a while longer.

Winyo couldn't fathom the reason why somebody or anybody would want to live in a community that so openly resented them. It was not like this family didn't have other options. They were clearly wealthy, judging by the gigantic Range Rover Winyo had glimpsed, parked at the side of the house.

Usually, the villagers helped one another in doing tasks such as house arrangement, especially when a family had been away for so long. Their absence at the Odyek residence made Winyo wonder why the family could not take a hint.

Winyo felt sorry for them. That was what she felt instead of the wide-eyed fear that her friend Acholla often adapted when speaking about the Odyek family.

It had to be sad, having people hate you, Winyo thought. She could not stand it when people spoke ill of her. She couldn't even begin to imagine what it felt like to have the entire village loathe the ground that you stepped on.

Winyo had seen the Odyek boys drive up to the market. Yes, she had. She saw almost everyone that went to the village centre. Her family shop was positioned along the dusty main road. Sometimes the Odyeks stopped to purchase flour and cereal from the shop.

There was nothing ordinary about the five boys and it had nothing to do with the rumors in the village. The Odyek brothers were a very handsome bunch. Yes, Winyo couldn't help the smile that lingered on her lips every time she thought of those tall impossibly handsome brothers. It was just not fair that they were so mercilessly good looking and fancy. Gosh, were they fancy! The village whispers and talk that went along with them only seemed to brush past them, like the gush of the wind that had the luxury to caress their skin. They talked and dressed decent, unlike the ordinary village boys she knew, who only dressed well when they wanted to get lucky.

Winyo's mother had once overheard her and Acholla talking about the physical attributes of the brothers and the woman had lost her ever-loving mind. She had flown into a tirade of how supernatural the looks of the boys were and that Winyo should keep away from their darkness, which brought them to the most recent village gossip. Apparently, Alice Odyek used some magic charm on her sons to keep them looking the way they did (which was: totally handsome), so as to lure the daughters of women in order to steal their souls. It had scared the breath out of Winyo when she first heard it. Later she concluded that the whole story seemed all too fanciful. Her mother talked too much.

Winyo decided not to pay much thought to that particular rumour. She was sure half the girls in the village with healthy hormones had done the same.

Right now, she and Acholla stood right behind one of them. His name was Guma Odyek. He was the middle son. He kept much to himself- they all did, but he was...intriguing. Winyo's mother would have used the words, 'extraordinarily weird.'

He had this quiet energy about him that seemed to vibrate and command attention. It was also this that made her hesitant to speak with him. She spoke to his brothers when they came to her shop but never to him. He rarely made attempts to speak to her either, but that didn't stop her silly heart from skipping several beats every time she saw him.

Sometimes when she came across him on the road, her tongue seemed to forget how to function properly as well, muttering something that could have been, 'How do you do?' in gabbled unintelligible jumbles.

He always answered something, but she was always too deaf with inexplicable fear to hear. Nothing seemed to function properly when she was around that particular Odyek. Perhaps it was his fault. The talk about the family was quickly veering towards him and the village fear was always infectious. Winyo had come to the firm conclusion that this was the cause of her discomfort around him.

One time she was riding past him, and he had waved at her and she had nearly fallen off her bicycle. Thus, Winyo had given up on greeting him completely, but for some bizarre reason she happened to meet him more often than usual lately. This, all the more, made her rounds of flour deliveries feel more numerous than usual, which was ridiculous.

Her mother had later on corrupted her with a story, that when a witch's son is walking on the same path as you and he happens to wave, it is best to give way, in respect to the spirit that protected him, and also so that the spirit could find no fault with you.

It was nonsense, Winyo knew that much. She was educated for goodness' sake! But still she always slid off her bicycle whenever she crossed Guma's path, and the distance she maintained was definitely the epitome of respect.

Yes, she hated herself for doing this and vowed each time that it would never happen again- but of course she did it again and again and again. She was a hopeless coward at times.

Crouching under the shrubs now, Winyo pondered at the wisdom of her decision to follow her friend to spy on Guma. Winyo always wondered whether Alice was really a witch and if so, what her intentions were. They couldn't all be bad. She had heard of witches that provided spiritual help to people. There were so many witch doctors that she had come across from her bicycle rides to the other clan villages, but none of them looked like Alice.

Alice was reserved, well put-together and decent; the type of woman who could be referred to as a lady or a 'real' woman, like the people in her village referred to a good woman.

"We should not be here," Winyo whispered now, as she crept behind Acholla whose only response was tightening the grip on her hand and farther dragging her through the shrubs.

"Don't you want to know?" she hissed.

Winyo knew what she meant. Translated, it meant, *"didn't she want to be the first with the newest gossip about the queer family?"*

"Let's leave him alone," Winyo whispered. They were only a few paces behind him, and she could hear the soft scratches of pencil on paper as he worked on, seemingly oblivious to their presence.

"What do you think he is doing?" Acholla whispered.

"Drawing," Winyo hissed back. Guma was the weirdest of the brothers and if her curiosity was taking her anywhere, it would not be to him. She didn't like to admit this, even to herself, but Guma freaked her out as much as he intrigued her.

"Go away," he spoke suddenly, and Winyo tensed in surprise. His back was still turned to them, his head bent low to near chest level. His voice was a near sigh that had her wondering whether it was to them that he had been speaking.

It was not the first time that she had heard him speak. His voice was like the dry rustle of the leaves in the wind, simple yet strangely extraordinary, carrying the strength of honesty bordering the dark allure of a secret. Gosh, there went her heart again, missing another beat; he always managed to elicit this response in her.

Before either of them could react, he was on his feet and in a surprise agile leap, he vaulted over a rock and towards them, then tore at the shrub they were huddled under.

In an instant, Winyo felt like she had shrunk ten feet as she realized with dizzying terror and clarity at the mocking proximity that he had been to them.

He was a tall young man, but he definitely seemed to tower to the sky right now as he stood before them. She stared in frozen awe and terror at him. His shirt flapped wildly with the wind as the length of the high grasses waved behind him, making the whole situation all the more dramatic and surreal. This was when her lungs refused to work as well…air…Winyo thought dazedly. She couldn't breathe. Her knees weakened and her heart took flight. Acholla beside her was every inch as terrified as she was. Winyo had a trembling hand on her shoulder to prove that.

"What do you want?" he demanded.

Acholla's hardening grip on her shoulder was no doubt a signal for her to speak up. Winyo wanted to swear and she did so in her mind. Acholla always got her into situations.

"Are you deaf?" he snarled.

The tone snapped her out of her haze of panic. "What are you doing here?"

"Nothing that should concern you," he snapped. "Leave."

Yeah, she hated that tone, it grated on her nerves. Grappling at the tattered hems of her dignity, Winyo rose up to her full height and craned her slender neck to add on a few inches. It didn't make much of a difference though; he was much taller than she was. Everyone was much taller than she was, but if he was handing out orders, she would rather not take them crouching beneath his feet.

She was short at 5′2″. It was a height that no one failed to notice, especially in a community where people towered regally into the sky like it was some freakish competition. It did not help either that she was called Winyo, which in Acholli meant 'bird.'

Yes, her height and her name had been subjected to jokes and ridicule so much so that she had grown to hate them both. Some people called her 'daughter of Ader,' which was preferable to her. Ader was her mother.

Guma was exceptionally tall, like all Acholli men were. All she could judge of Guma was that his height was probably right for his age, which was in the range of nineteen and twenty. He did not possess the typical Acholli facial features, in that his nose was long, firm and exquisitely narrow with square cheek bones.

Where most Acholli men were as dark as she, he was of light complexion. The gods must have spent extra time chiseling his cheek bones; he was breathtakingly beautiful. She could look at him forever... but the feeling wasn't mutual. His eyes returned her scrutiny with a hot hard glare that would melt the wax off a candle.

"You cannot tell us to leave," Winyo feebly attempted to stand her ground. "We can go wherever we like."

"You are here to watch me."

"Urh..." she spat defensively as she groped for sane reasons to explain their presence. Finding none, she continued, "Such- such nerve. Why would I even do something like that? We don't even know you."

A spark lit up in his eyes and he looked half amused as he intently studied her face. "Perhaps you are here to get to know me then," he drawled lazily.

Winyo gaped at him, her mouth running dry. His tone implied other things besides the surface meaning of those words. Other darker, sensual things. Or was that her dirty mind? Was he being sarcastic?

Gosh! She didn't know.

He drew her out of her confused thoughts when he said, "You seem harmless, but I still want you to leave."

"It-it is not like I want to be anywhere near you," she managed to say. "We were just passing by."

"Really?" This time the amusement lit up his entire gorgeous face as he glanced around their bush. "What are you doing here then?"

Lifting her chin up she said, "That is none of your business."

He laughed this time and nodded. "I still would prefer it if you left."

Somehow this made her feel even worse - being politely dismissed and sent on her way. It annoyed her immensely considering that she had not wanted to be in this situation in the first place. Clutching Acholla's hand, she stomped away, half dragging her friend behind her. They both stumbled a good number of times through the high grass without complaint.

No words were necessary, they both just wanted to get out of there as fast as they could. There was indeed something darkly scary and alluring about Guma. No wonder the villagers said he was bizarre. Some had begun to say that of all the brothers, it was he who had taken most to his mother's 'side of the family.' For a second, she found herself pondering how much truth the village rumors held about this young man.

Back on the road, they clambered onto their bicycles and were riding out of there as fast as the old metals could take them. They rode for a long distance before they slowed down. Then looking at each other, they both burst into laughter at the release of pent-up tension. They laughed till tears rolled down their cheeks. Their voices tingling with girlish mirth, echoing down the empty road, joined by the chirp of the evening birds.

"*Jal*," Acholla said in Acholli, "Guma clearly did not want us there." Wiping the tears from her eyes, Acholla clambered back on her bicycle and started to pedal. Winyo followed suit. "What do you think he was hiding?"

"*Jal*, I only saw as much as you did," Winyo replied, using the same reference that her friend had applied to her; *Jal*, meaning 'buddy' in Acholli. "It only seemed like he was drawing."

"Or waiting for something to happen. He couldn't have been that rude if he was just *drawing*," Acholla insinuated. "We have to tell the girls about this."

The girls as Acholla put it were their close friends, the identical twins Apio and Acen. Those two were so close that it was rare to find one in any place without the other. They had a strange way of finishing each other's sentences without irritating a listener, which uncannily created a feeling of listening to one person speak, instead of two giggling girls. The twins were far worse gossips than her and Acholla combined yet they somehow got away with it.

"What exactly are we telling them?" Winyo asked.

"That we saw him doing one of his witch practices."

Winyo glanced sharply at her. "When did we see him do that?"

"Come on, you don't believe you saw him just drawing, did you?"

"What? I am sorry, what else did you see him do?" She was stunned.

"Winyo, there was something there. That was why he didn't want us there. Did you notice that he didn't need to turn around to realize we were there? He spoke before he saw us."

Winyo had to agree with that but… "He could have heard us make a sound."

"*Jal*, we didn't make any sound, but even so, there are a number of things that make noise in the bush but we don't necessarily assume them to be people, now do we?"

Again, she was right, and Winyo was fast finding it hard not to think along Acholla's lines.

"It is a shame that he is not as good looking as his brothers though,"

Acholla added breathlessly as she pedaled.

Winyo glanced sharply at her friend. Obviously, the fellow was good looking, but Winyo was not about to disagree with Acholla. Instead, she said, "He is the middle son. The middle children always have issues, and he clearly has a lot."

"They all have issues," Acholla said in conclusion of the topic of the Odyek family. They had just reached the road that forked off to Acholla's home. They said quick goodbyes and she was fast pedaling on her way home. The Odyek son momentarily forgotten, Winyo went into a battle with her conscience for allowing Acholla to come on this trip with her. She was usually slow when making distant deliveries to shops, but with Acholla around, she turned into a snail.

Acholla's family did not sell cereals like her family did. So, there was really no need to have their daughter ride through miles of land to make deliveries to the shops and village trade centres. Lucky for Winyo, recently, on her return from school, her parents had secured specific shops where she had to deliver the cereals and the flour. So, in this school holiday, Winyo and her mother no longer had to sleep over for days away from home during a trade week. All she had to do was merely deliver to shops and be on her way back home.

It was a good thing, but everything came with disadvantages. One of them was that her mother blew her top whenever Winyo got back home late- which was all the time.

She could not ride as fast as her mother and did not have her stamina so she always got home after dark. This was not that bad, but her mother always wanted her daughter to make supper for the family. That was the real reason she was always pissed off.

It was the downside of being an only daughter. She was the second child and only daughter of Ader's four children. In the Acholli tribe, such girls usually had special names; they were called Ayaa or Afule. She, on the other hand, was named Winyo.

By now the pet name Ayaa should have been adopted, but clearly everyone liked her name more than she did, considering her futile attempts at talking her friends into calling her Ayaa.

It had been infuriating how names like 'shortie,' 'ground height' and 'small,' always stuck to her. But good old times had imparted her with the knowledge that the more she hated them, the more they were used. With time the names stopped. They still called her 'small' though.

Right now, Winyo could picture with almost precision the scenario at home. Her brothers were probably already home, doing nothing, as usual, waiting for her to come and prepare supper while her mother was going on about how lazy her daughter was. Her father, well, he had the punishment of listening to his wife.

Winyo didn't complain. Her mother had a reason for needing her at home. Ader had recently given birth, another son. Now there were three sons, which meant, three useless brothers. Her father had been overjoyed at the recent birth of the fourth child, Amone. Winyo had been devastated.

She didn't hate her brothers. No, she did not. She loved them. Sometimes. She wanted a sister a lot more, you know, someone to share her mother's insults with. Her mother only kept the good words and compliments for her brothers.

Her older brother Apach and the other Otim helped with the farming; it was just among the few contributions they made to ease her life. Sometimes they helped her and her mother at the shop, but most of the time they didn't really do anything.

A lot of the time, they were away with their father making visits to friends and searching for local herbs which nobody really bought. They spent hours away from home.

Winyo's home was at the far end of the village, surrounded with grass so high that the nearest neighbors' homes were barely visible. However, the compound at Winyo's home was always well kept, she made certain of that. The homestead consisted of four well-built grass thatched huts. Her parents slept in the largest hut that had the walls decorated in white and yellow zigzag patterns. Winyo had the duty of ensuring that they were kept in their bright well- painted state.

One thing that Winyo was glad for was that she no longer had to share the same hut with her brothers. She had her own hut, and it was the smallest of the four. It had been built behind the one that her brothers now shared.

Their uncle Orach and his wife Atang lived in the hut closest to her parents' and it was the same hut that also served as the kitchen sometimes. Winyo hated cooking in the kitchen. There was always too much soot from the firewood, and it made her eyes run.

It had become so bad that at one point she was unable to see clearly for a week. Her father had dug a hole beside the kitchen and arranged it with three cooking stones for her kitchen use.

Her eyes cleared with time, but she no longer cooked from inside the kitchen unless it was absolutely necessary, which was annoyingly often in the rainy season. A particular burden considering that her older brother and her father had different tastes in food and occasionally disagreed on what they wanted to eat and, when this happened, her mother would have her prepare two sets of meals which had to be presented to the royal of royals at the same time. Darn them!

Winyo shook her head, the thought of having to go through that ordeal with meals today crawled through her mind like a dying bug. She almost slowed her pace but one glance at the darkening sky sent her pumping harder at the bicycle pedals.

Usually, when she didn't have the physical strength to finish up something (which was often), she tabled out debates in her head to convince herself that whatever it was that she was rushing probably wasn't all that important.

Right now, as she guided the bicycle to their compound, her mother bellowing her name was the first homely sound that blared through the homestead like a war call.

"Winyo! Winyo?!!" The woman was clearly in a temper. "Winyo, is that you?"

Winyo suddenly felt so exhausted that she wished for the luxury of not answering back. "Yes, Mama," she answered, "It is I."

Her mother emerged from behind one of the huts, carrying the baby at her side. In her other hand she held a basket full of vegetables that she had been sorting.

"Winyo!" she screeched, her voice even louder, "Did Pajule become longer than its usual distance?"

"No, Ma—"

"Then what kept you so long? You go about dragging yourself like the thing that old people don't like. You know you have to get home early!" she yelled, shifting the baby from one side to the other.

Winyo knew it was a matter of seconds before the baby would start screaming. It usually did, saving her from the trouble of having to listen to their mother. She was counting on that now, as she busied herself tying the bicycle against the support hold of one of the huts.

"Did you not find Odoch?!" Ader demanded.

"He was not there when I first arrived, I had to wait," Winyo lied. Odoch, the person whom she had been delivering millet to in Pajule had been there alright. He had been waiting for her for quite a while before she had arrived. He had given her near about the same lecture about being late as her mother was about to do now.

"I found that he had just gone to a meeting with someone, somewhere and had left a young boy in attendance at the shop. He didn't know anything about the millet that I was delivering," Winyo continued lying like a bandit. She always had an excuse for everything, but she unfortunately gave unnecessarily long explanations when lying. It was easier to omit the truth than have her mother go on at her for being lazy. That was just one thing that she was not.

She worked extraordinarily hard, but just a little slower than she would have liked or slower than her mother would have liked.

"Did he give you the money?" Ader attacked, but before Winyo could answer, she went off with another round of words. "...Do not tell me you lost the money on the way. Girls come up with stories like that these days so that they can steal money. You do that to me, I swear." She made a florid motion of touching the ground and sweeping her arm in a full out circle to point at the sky, in a superfluous yet effective display of an oath to the gods. "You do that, Winyo...do that to me and I will show you who your mother is."

Winyo fumbled in the inside of her pockets and drew out the small piece of cloth that she usually tied money in. That way she wouldn't lose it. Her mother had warned her on numerous occasions about losing money that she literally triple check her pockets each time.

"Is it all here?!" Ader barked as Winyo brought the money to her. Winyo nodded, and as if on cue, her baby brother opened his mouth and let out a yowl so loud that one would think that he was being tortured.

"Here, hold him," Ader said as she dumped the baby in her arms, and the vegetables followed. That was her send off to the kitchen.

Winyo just couldn't understand why her mother had had the insane need to have another child considering three were already too much to handle. Frankly, she couldn't understand why people boasted about having so many children. It only meant more noise, more migraines and more work.

Her father had made a fire in the middle of the compound and he and his brother Orach were sitting on low chairs while drinking the local brew from calabashes. As usual, Orach's wife, Atang was not at home. It was always a wonder to her where that woman was at the late evening hours.

Atang always returned late at night. She always had stories about visiting relatives and friends and all that garbage that Winyo did not buy. She often wondered how dumb her uncle had to be to believe a thing that came out of her mouth. Atang was a certified liar.

Sure, the home could get boring at times, but Atang usually left home in the late afternoons; her trips were becoming more frequent as of late. Honestly it didn't bother her one bit that her uncle chose to remain as dumb as duck. What bothered her more was Atang's reluctance to help with the household work. That was why people had aunties, right? To help. Well, hers was useless.

Barging into the kitchen with the baby at her side, she paused to give gratitude to whoever had lit the kerosene lamp in the kitchen. She stomped around for the saucepans and the knives, all the while trying to hush the baby whose shrill screams were reaching feverous pitch.

The jerrycans were empty which meant no water in the kitchen. Winyo cursed under her breath. Her younger brother Otim had not fetched the water as she had instructed. *The jerk!* She was going to kill him.

Winyo opened the door to take a peek at the sky. It was already dark. She cursed again. The borehole was miles away and she was too afraid of the dark to contemplate going. It would take about an hour to get there and back. Her mother would surely give her a beating tonight if she didn't wise up and get some water for cooking and for the baby.

She mulled over going to the home of one of the neighbors to ask for water, but Odur's family had as many useless boys as hers and Aket's family was too big for her to even consider borrowing anything from them.

Acholla, the name floated to her like a life-saving raft. Acholla's house was not far away, and her family consisted of a number of girls.

They had jerrycans of water to spare.

In her arms, the baby had graduated from screaming to making choked gaggling howls. Winyo frowned as she searched around the old hut. She wanted to stuff something in his mouth, anything to stop that awful irritating sound.

In haste, she made the fire and started the meal, tying the whimpering baby to her back. She grabbed one of the jerrycans and debated with herself how she was going to make it past her father with the baby on her back. After further hesitation, she eventually stuffed a pacifier in his mouth and shut him up. That would not last long.

Winyo slipped behind the house and within minutes was racing along the bushy path, Acholla's house was a lot closer that way.

"Winyo?" someone called out her name. Startled at the introduction of the new voice, she slowed down but still continued to walk. She knew who it was. It was Okeny, one of her brother's friends. He was a lanky fellow, dark in complexion. His face was narrow, but with sharp, angled cheek bones that had the effect of making his face crow like. She did not like him.

"How did you see me?" she asked, as he caught up with her and kept pace.

"What's the rush?"

"How did you see me?" she asked again. It was so dark that the only way he would have known it was her was if he had been watching the kitchen door- which he did all the time when he visited and she detested it eternally.

He was always watching her like a hawk, his eyes trailing her, leering over every curve, like it was his path to salvation. She always ignored him, but there were times, like this that he was impossible to shake off. As much as she was afraid of the dark and needed company, his company was particularly irksome.

"I came to visit your brother and was leaving when I saw you scampering away into the dark."

"What? Di- did my brother see me?" Her heart raced; she would be in more trouble that way.

"No, he didn't. Do you have something to hide?"

"No," she snapped crossly.

"Where are you going?" he demanded. The touch of possessiveness in his tone grated at her frayed nerves. "Is it a man you are going to meet?"

Is it a man? Winyo scowled into the dark, seized with the impulse to hit at something, preferably, Okeny. Words could not possibly explain how much she resented him. She felt her skin crawl every time he touched her, an action that he enjoyed doing, and her senses repelled it like water did oil.

"Just don't tell my brother you saw me," Winyo said tightly.

"So, it is a man," he concluded harshly.

"No, it is not, for goodness' sake!" she yelled in exasperation. "I need water, and there is no water in the house."

"Likely story. You expect me to believe that you are going to fetch water at this time of the night?" he asked in obvious disbelief. "The borehole is miles away."

Winyo couldn't restrain the growl that pushed through her teeth. "Well, if you must know, I am not going to the borehole."

"I already guessed that."

"I am going to Acholla's house," Winyo labored on. There was a long pause in which she figured that he was verifying the amount of truth in her words as if she needed his permission to do anything.

"Okay," he said in conclusion. "I will walk with you."

She wished he wouldn't. "If it will keep you from telling my brother that you met me tonight, then come along," Winyo reluctantly agreed. They were some distance away from Acholla's home now.

"So," he began, "how come you don't have water in the home?"

Winyo sighed deeply, now that they had established that he was going to dog guard her all the way. She was rather hoping they would walk in silence, but such miracles were as rare as hen's teeth.

"Winyo?" He was waiting.

"I had gone very far to deliver millet," she explained in a rush of words. "I didn't get the chance to finish some house chores."

"You usually do that before you leave." He panted on beside her, the fellow consumed air like a vortex. "You usually are very efficient, what happened this time?"

Usually? How Winyo wished her mind didn't immediately note the choice of his words. This guy was fast graduating from the annoying admirer to a psycho stalker. Neither were exactly comforting thoughts when alone in the dark with the individual in question.

"It doesn't matter." She brushed him off.

"Doesn't matter? Doesn't matter?!" His voice was pitching. "How can you say something like that?"

"What?"

"You coming back to fetch water in the dark. You say it doesn't matter?!" he raged on. Winyo could not fathom why he was getting angry; it wasn't like it was any of his business how she did her chores.

He was still speaking. "You know what I think?"

No, she really was way too exhausted to even sustain this conversation.

"…you wanted to meet someone tonight, didn't you?"

"Okeny," she sighed in exasperation. "Be quiet."

She picked up her pace. She could see the lights from Acholla's home compound some distance ahead.

"Who is it?" he demanded.

"Okeny, are you drunk?"

"Winyo, do not take that tone with me." She could almost see him point a finger at her in the semi darkness. "I will not stand to have you sneaking around with people who do not have good intentions."

Supposedly he did. "I am just going to get water," Winyo stressed. Acholla's home was so close now, and the strides she was taking were as brisk as running paces.

"So, you really didn't fetch water before you left?"

She wanted to scream in frustration but thankfully they got to Acholla's house before he had gone off into another tangent.

Winyo managed to convince Acholla and her sister Perima to accompany her back home. Okeny tagged along of course. They parted ways with her some short distance from her home.

Winyo had just made it to the compound, when her baby brother, having kept quiet for far too long, opened his demanding mouth and let out one of those shrill animal-like shrieks.

Her mother emerged at once from one of the huts and immediately spotted her at the entrance of the compound. "Winyo…!"

2

"*Jal, Icoo maber*?" Acen greeted. It was morning and the twins Acen and Apio had stopped by Winyo's shop on the way to the borehole. They were standing outside the shop restlessly swaying their jerrycans.

As usual, they were wearing identical clothing. Today they made a sight in floral patterned short dresses. Their long hair was combed out in a loose style that perfectly framed their round cheeky beauty, emphasizing their identical long lashes and wide startling brown eyes.

"You seem mighty cheery," Winyo replied without enthusiasm as she dragged herself about the small shop arranging the bags of cereal and flour. She was feeling extremely lazy- she usually felt that way in the early hours of the morning. Her arms felt like two heavy rocks as she pulled the high chair to the counter and perched on it like a dying cockerel. She was not a morning person.

Winyo peered up at the twins as she started the task of measuring flour in weights and securing them in polythene packages. It was an activity she performed nearly every morning. Her mother had gone to the fields after informing her that she wouldn't be coming to the shop today. She had taken the baby with her- *thank the spirits*.

"It's a new morning," Apio chirped.

Acen added with gusto, 'Opete is getting married.'

From behind the shop counter Winyo paused, her cloudy mind

trying to register this information. Opete...wasn't he the uncle of somebody she knew? Wait- wasn't he the drunk her mother beat up months back? Winyo struggled to clear her mind as she dusted the flour spray from her face. Most days she was unrecognizable by the time she finished measuring the flour.

"*Jal*, where did you hear that from?" Winyo asked skeptically. Yes, she remembered now- Opete was a relative to the Odyek family.

"It is everywhere," Apio replied as she hopped onto the outer cement counter of her shop window. "He announced it yesterday to his mates when they were drinking."

"Yeah, our Abaa told us," Acen said as she noisily placed a jerrycan on the ground and hopped onto the counter as well.

The twins, like most children in their village, referred to their father as 'Abaa,' something that Winyo had been unable to do. Her father hated the word and had insisted that she refer to him as Daddy as soon as she had learnt to speak. He claimed that it sounded more modern that way, and he was a modern man.

Winyo now nodded with interest at the news being conveyed to her. Opete was one of the relatives of the Odyek family. He was a common drunk who talked so much that it was hard not to like him. He was very friendly, perhaps that was why his connection to the Odyek family had been overlooked. Winyo hadn't even known he was related to that family until their sudden appearance in town.

"Who is he marrying?"

"Penina, Oleyo's daughter," Acen answered, "They have been seeing each other for quite a while now, lucky girl, right?'

Winyo resisted the urge to laugh. *Lucky girl*? Marrying a man who drank too much didn't seem like a good choice for a partner. Secondly, the whole Odyek-ness of the situation was bothersome. Much as Winyo liked to lie to herself that she didn't believe in the whole witchcraft hullabaloo, there was still no way that she would marry into a family rumored to indulge in the dark arts.

"Why is she marrying him?" Winyo asked absently. That had the girls bursting into peals of laughter. Only then did she realize how inappropriate and rude the question had sounded.

"Sour much?" Apio giggled.

"No—" Winyo sighed in resignation, "I had a terrible evening."

"What could have been so bad that even the talk of a wedding couldn't brighten you up?" Acen queried.

"Okeny," Winyo spat, the name burning her tongue. "He followed me around all night."

"What?" came the identical chorus, the excitement in their tones palpable. Winyo rolled her eyes. "He only followed me to make sure that it was indeed just water that I was in search for in the dark of the evening."

"Something is going down with you and Okeny?" Apio teased. "He seems to be everywhere that you are."

Boy did she know that!

Acen spoke, "What was the deal with you going to Acholla's house? Can't blame Okeny for questioning your motives."

Winyo's eyes drifted from one twin to the other. "You have already spoken to Acholla? She told me that they were leaving for one of their far-off fields first thing in the morning."

"The others did. Acholla left after them," Apio answered.

Acen added, "She will not be dropping by your shop this afternoon, in case you were wondering."

"Uh-huh, so about last night? Where were you really going?" Apio leaned in as she playfully batted her lashes.

"You too? Come on." Winyo shook her head.

"Acholla told us you showed up at her place with Okeny, so..." Apio nudged on.

"*Jal*, stop it, you know I don't like him," Winyo said as she finished up with the last pack of flour. "There is no secret there."

"But why don't you like him?" Apio persisted.

Acen joined in like she usually did. "The guy is so handsome, who wouldn't want him?"

Winyo shook her head in surrender. The twins were just trying to get a story out of her to gossip about at the borehole. Okeny could be called a lot of things, but good looking was not one of them. He had missed the look good cloud by a very, very long yard stick. Everyone in the village said Okeny was a nice boy. Winyo often found herself searching for that rare quality in the guy in question. Perhaps if he always didn't manage to successfully annoy her with every conversation that they held, she might have glimpsed the beauty in him. She may have even *liked* him…urgh that thought made her throw up a little in her mouth.

"I just don't like him," she said eventually.

"Are you playing hard to get?" Apio pressed on, "Because if you are, you are playing the game too hard."

"You and Okeny think alike. The two of you should just hook up," Winyo muttered crossly as the twins burst into their identical laughter. They had this routine of laughter where they spun round in a smart circle, twirling their hands in the air, all the while their mirth graduating with musical pitch, finally ending with a whoop and a high five clap above their heads.

Winyo stifled a groan. It was way too early in the morning for this kind of energy.

"You two are mighty happy today," Winyo commented dryly.

"Come on, *Small*, it's a good day, you should lighten up."

Small. Those two were adopting that name again? She was doomed. "I will be happy once I finish my rounds of cereal delivery."

"How many of those are you left with?" Acen asked.

"Not many, unless some people in the other villages send orders to my father."

The twins started going about fussing with each other's hair, no doubt getting ready to continue their journey to the borehole. Oh goody, Winyo thought, she could catch a nap as soon as they took their cheeriness to the borehole.

"Okay, we have to leave now…" Apio began their goodbyes, as she straightened the belt on her sister's dress.

"We will be back to see you in the evening if you are still here," Acen added, "Acholla certainly won't be around today. We shall pass by and update you on the latest news in the village centre."

"But we can still stay awhile, here, with you," Apio added.

What now? Winyo, who had her head down checking the sale records, looked up in surprise at the clutter of plastic on the ground as the twins dropped their jerrycans. She didn't have to wonder for long.

Acen was giggling, "Yeah just for a little while. What's the rush?"

The enormous Range Rover belonging to the Odyek family had just parked at the dusty roadside right in front of Winyo's family shop. The car made a sight as it stood menacingly like an attacking bull on the road. This was the main road that led to the village center which was a short distance away. It was early morning, so there were quite a number of people on the road walking up to the village center. Their attention of course was taken by the brothers, who were alighting from the car like formidable gods stepping out of the heavens. The tension in the air was palpable as the twins fidgeted with excitement.

There were four of them. Okwera, the youngest, Paul, the eldest, Ernest, the second eldest and finally the Odyek she couldn't seem to get her mind off, Guma, last to get out of the car. His gaze immediately locked with hers; Winyo hastily looked away as her palms began to sweat. She turned to the twins and said, "You want to talk with them?"

"Doesn't every girl?" Acen whispered.

The four of them strolled over to the shop, exuding raw male confidence as captivating as it was intimidating. They were tall, and together they appeared to be almost the same height. Only Okwera was shorter than the rest, which was probably because he was the youngest.

They all shared the same thick, dark hair, but unlike the light skinned Guma, the others were of a darker complexion. The brothers looked alike, with almost identical square cut chins, thin lips and perfectly narrow nose. Yes, alike, yet different and the traits potently gave varying effects on the different faces. Winyo's breath lodged somewhere in her lungs and her heart was doing that weird speeding thing it always did around them. They were all positively drooling by the time the brothers were at the shop.

Paul was the first to speak to Winyo, flashing her a dazzling smile which was meant to charm her, but Winyo was almost positive that she experienced a near heart attack in that moment.

"How are you today?"

"Fine, how may we help you?" the twins chimed. *Bless their identical hearts.*

"Are you twins?" Okwera asked, his attention drawn by Acen and Apio, who were openly ogling them. Who could blame them? When it came to the Odyek boys, there was certainly a lot to be ogled.

"Yes," they replied and went on ahead to introduce themselves as Earnest made an order for maize flour and fresh beans.

"You girls live around here?" Earnest asked of the twins as he was done with the orders. Winyo didn't know what it was about twins, but she was yet to find a society that did not find them intriguing. These twins in particular knew their appeal and prettily tossed their neatly done hair and batted their pretty little lashes like shy brides. For a moment that didn't last more than a minute, Winyo experienced a burst of jealousy at the attention being directed at her friends. If she were to die, she wanted to come back as one of those twins. They had it all, they were pretty, educated, their parents doted over them, and the entire village loved them. Not to mention that the boys in the village looked at them with heart shaped eyes.

Did Guma think they were intriguing? Winyo found herself wondering. What did she care anyway? It was not like he would ever be interested in the likes of her. She was not particularly pretty, but she wasn't ugly either. She was just a short, safely plain, mildly interesting but mostly shy village girl. Yeah, she was forgettable. She would have loved to be loud and outgoing like the twins, but the courage always failed her. So, she kept on performing her duty behind the counter.

"Are you two new here?" Earnest continued. Winyo had to resist the urge to laugh. The twins were practically celebrities in the village.

"No, we are not new, we are from this village," Apio said.

"I am kicking myself right now for not being able to notice girls like you," Paul said. The girls broke into giggles. *Oh, how adorable,* Winyo thought wryly as she buried herself behind the counter, making a mental note to learn a few things from those ever-so-cheery two.

By the time she emerged with the weighed and packed fresh beans, the conversation had veered to the evening music dancing that occurred at the village centre.

"Winyo, who owns that music system?" Apio asked her as Winyo placed the weight stones on the counter for measurement.

Winyo tried to focus her attention on carefully filling a thin polythene package with the millet flour that they had ordered. She was battling with her nerves; this was the first time that all the Odyek brothers had come to her shop. She couldn't help but wonder if it had something to do with her sneaking up on Guma. Oh gosh! Were they angry with her? Struggling to make her movements appear fluid, Winyo tried to focus on her task.

"It is owned by Tomas; don't you know him? The man who moved here from Sudan. He is a Dinka," Winyo said in reply to Apio's question.

"You mean the Dinka who drives the beat up grey, double cabin Toyota?" Guma spoke. Once again her heart forgot a beat, and the measuring cup slipped from her hand, spilling the rest of the flour on the counter. It was at that moment that the wind chose to change direction and spray the flour fully into her face. She stumbled back, coughing and spluttering.

"Are- are you okay?" Okwera asked, leaning over as she struggled to clean her eyes.

"Yes," she huffed, hurriedly bending to retrieve the cup. She couldn't seem to function correctly where Guma was concerned. Maybe he really was a witch doctor.

"Are you sure?" Paul asked with concern. Winyo nodded. She slid a glance at Guma. Where his brothers had moved in to be of unneeded assistance, as men usually did, Guma still shadowed the same spot he had darkened since his arrival, his hands buried deep inside his pockets, his eyes studying her.

Just after making sure Winyo was okay, all attention turned back to the twins. "So, you girls going to the dances?" Paul asked, his gaze sliding appreciatively over the twins. The girls tittered as they both shook their heads in reply, leaning seductively against the counter. Honestly, Winyo hadn't even known it was possible to make her dusty counter seem enticing.

Earnest was saying, "That is such a shame, bodies like yours are meant for movement."

'All kinds of movement,' Paul emphasized, male appreciation lacing his tone like well fermented wine. Winyo's mouth nearly watered at the images his words conjured in her mind.

Okwera said, "We all obviously would love to go to the dances but only if you gorgeous girls came with us. It would be a tragedy not to have at least one dance with either of you, or both of you, at the same time."

The girls giggled with obvious pleasure.

"Stop scaring the girls," chided Earnest. "We wouldn't want them to think we are total cave men." The Odyek brothers definitely knew how to flirt. For the tenth time that morning, Winyo found herself longing to be the focus of this overt male interest.

"We go dancing sometimes, but only if our brothers take us," Apio replied.

Acen added, "We are not allowed to go anywhere in the dark without them."

"Hmmm... Any chance we could take you and act brotherly for the night?" Earnest teased.

"You don't even know how to be a brother?" Paul cut in.

"Shut your trap Paul," Earnest snapped good naturedly as everyone burst into laughter.

Winyo managed a smile as she went back to her work. She slid a glance at Guma. He still stood where he had been when they had arrived, his attention fixed on her.

"What of you?" Guma spoke, his eyes never leaving hers. "Do you go to the dance?"

Words...words, Winyo thought wildly, her stomach twisted in wild knots. "I- I don't go," she stammered.

"Why on earth not?" Okwera asked.

"I am too busy."

Guma looked like he was about to say something, but Earnest cut in by saying, "I don't think it would be a good idea for us to attend any dance here."

Indeed, Winyo had to agree with him, the Odyeks would have to be crazier than the village mad man if they thought their attendance would go unnoticed. The villagers would most likely close the dance prematurely upon their arrival and have everyone go home. Still, she said, "It's a shame, I hear the dances are usually fun."

"Are you truly too busy to attend?" Guma asked. Winyo knew the question was directed at her and once again, she avoided his gaze.

"My parents would never allow it, I have too much work to do at home."

"Can't you sneak out?" Guma asked insistently. "You look like the kind of girl who likes *sneaking around*."

This time she managed to keep eye contact. "I don't sneak around."

His lips twitched in amusement. "Could have fooled me. I usually don't like my privacy invaded, but I find myself making exceptions in certain circumstances."

The brothers looked from one to the other. "Are we missing something?" Okwera asked.

"Start talking you two," Paul tapped the counter. "What's happened?"

Winyo let her gaze drop, giving up the attempt at bravery. "Nothing happened," she muttered.

"Unfortunately," Guma added. His gaze snagged hers again and the whole world seemed to tilt at an axis. Was he flirting with her? No, it couldn't be, she thought hastily. It was just her wishful, attention starving mind longing hopelessly for an unattainable male. But the intensity in his eyes burned and seared through her like molten coal; her insides melted like butter.

"What is your name?" Guma asked and for a second, she was seized with the wrenching need to lie because it was at that exact moment that she realized that she liked him, like really liked him, like wanted to marry him and make little Odyek babies and ride off into the sunset nonsense. A jarring realization, considering that moments before she had thought marrying into his family was a bad life choice. Also, what an utterly stupid fantasy to entertain. He would never think of her in that way, none of the boys did, except Okeny. Gosh did she hate that guy!

"You do have a name, right?" Guma prompted.

"Yes," Winyo found herself snapping almost too loudly as she fidgeted with the polythene bag in her hands. For some reason tying a knot had grown ten times more complicated.

They were all waiting for her name. She let out a heavy sigh. "Winyo," she mumbled. As expected, everyone broke into laughter. Even the twins, as if this was news to them.

"It's a beautiful name," Paul said, struggling to keep a straight face as he took the goods from her hands. "It's not every day that someone hears a name like that."

"I think it is fitting," Guma spoke to her as his brothers turned to leave. "Birds are pretty and nice. Winyo suits you."

A compliment, how she wished he hadn't given one; she rarely got any from guys, and she already knew she would be basking in this one for a long time, and she had, even long after the brothers had left.

Home that evening was noisy with excitement. Her father as usual had made the evening fire in the middle of the compound and her Uncle Orach piled it high with firewood. Meanwhile her mother chattered on and on about the upcoming wedding and subsequently the dowry and family backgrounds. Ader created and discussed various scenarios, even those without any facts. Just listening to her would get one running to the Odyeks for some supernatural remedy.

"They say he is going to give ten cows as part of the dowry," Ader rambled on, "I mean, how true is that?" Not that she cared about it. "The Odyek family is rich. Goodness knows all those years of witchcraft comes in handy sometimes. They have been living in Kitgum all this time- that place is as expensive to live in as Kampala. Alice Odyek will be pitching in right? Right?"

"She has to be. I saw her with her brother-in-law sometime this morning. They must have been talking about the wedding," Winyo's father replied, his face barely visible as he coughed behind the white blankets of smoke that drifted from his mouth, like evil vapors from hell's chimney. Gildo, Winyo's father always smoked the pipe. He claimed that the cigarettes that her uncle smoked had less taste, and he was a man of great taste.

"She has to pitch in," Ader was saying. "We can only hope that they don't brew some spells to conjure up the dowry. Come to think of it, they could easily cast spells on people who attend the wedding. That family should have stayed in Kitgum."

"Uh-uh," her uncle Orach intoned. "How they hid in that town, I will never know. Do you know that some believed that they were living in Kampala?"

"I can believe that," Ader agreed with a sneer, "That city is filled with all kinds of people. Don't you see how the city traders act when they come here? So immoral."

Those occasions were rare when the traders came up-country, but Ader was one to know when they did. "They try to cheat you out of your money with their fast tongues and tricks. I have seen them, yes I have, those men that come to buy rice from here."

Winyo's father nodded in agreement with his wife. "Those people are thieves. I remember they tried to buy our rice for twenty-seven thousand shillings a sack instead of the usual twenty-eight."

"I tell you if we had not sent our daughter to sell in town and make it back here in time with the correct price, we would have lost everything," Ader agreed.

It would have saved me a lot of riding if you had just sold the damn rice, Winyo thought bemused as she trotted about the compound, rocking her baby brother to sleep.

"Five bags of millet will be given for the dowry, so they say," Uncle

Orach informed them.

"They say that? That- that's what they are saying?" Ader's excitement usually made her stutter. "Who was saying that? Where- where did you hear that from?"

"At the centre today," explained Uncle Orach. "There was this man who said he overheard Opete, the excited groom, talking about it with someone."

Ader was getting more worked up than a boiling kettle. She was on her knees with excitement. It didn't take a genius to see where this was going.

"Gildo," she spoke to her husband, "do you understand what this means?"

Winyo knew what it meant- no more bicycle rides to town or the other villages. Something directly benefiting her was going to come out of this wedding. She sidled closer to the group of adults.

"We should get them to buy the millet from us," her mother was saying, "...and all the other goods that they will need."

Winyo was in total agreement with that.

"We have to get someone to convince them to buy from us," Gildo said, "someone to speak on our behalf."

"Why on earth would we do something like that?" Ader belted out the same question on Winyo's mind. Her father was a lot of things, but he was truly not the sharpest nail in the toolbox.

"We shall go talk to them ourselves," Ader continued, "Give them a fair price. We don't want someone saying the wrong things about us and giving them reasons not to trade with us."

"They may want to pay a lower price if we were to do that," said Gildo in an effort to redeem himself. "See, if we had someone to casually suggest to them that we offer fair prices, they would come and ask."

"No, they will not," Ader argued, "I am going to talk with Opete tomorrow."

"And tell him what?" Gildo argued, "That you suddenly forgot that you beat him senseless the last time that he failed to pay for the maize flour that you traded to him?"

Winyo cringed. That was a set-back. Even she had forgotten the incident. Her mother always involved herself in village fights and squabbles, it was hard to keep up with all of them.

One thing for certain was that Ader was never pleasant with those that failed to pay for what they got from the shop. Usually if they failed to pay, Ader's only compromise would be to barter, with vegetables or groundnut paste or chicken, depending on the quantity of what they took. But if that failed, she always beat the living daylights out of her debtors. Opete had unfortunately been one of those debtors.

"Come on don't exaggerate," Ader brushed off, her hands flying about in the air like this would wipe the incident out of memory. "It is not like I beat him; it was just a slap on the face."

Winyo tried hard not to chuckle, her mother's memory was so selective, it was often comical.

"Well, you slapped his dignity right out of him," Gildo said in amusement.

"In front of the entire neighborhood," Uncle Orach added.

"It was *nothing* and it happened a very long time ago. He is probably over it by now," Ader continued nonchalantly, but knowing her mother, Winyo caught the uncertainty in her voice. Well, she hoped for her own sake that indeed it was 'nothing' like her mother put it.

"Maybe we could soften him up by giving him something first," Uncle Orach suggested, "like a chicken, as congratulations for his wedding, before we start talking business."

"That is a clever idea," Ader agreed. Then she was back to her old commanding self. "Gildo, tomorrow you are going out to drink at the center."

"What?"

"You are going to talk to Opete first, since we all agree that me speaking with him wouldn't be a good start for us."

Gildo obviously didn't want to go, but trust Ader to be persuasive when she wanted to be. It didn't take long for the issue to be settled. Gildo was to attend the evening drinking place at the village centre to talk to Opete.

This was the sole reason as to why Ader spent the next day at the shop with Winyo. It was closer to the village centre than their home. Ader had set the whole day to wait for Opete's response even though they both knew it would be sometime until sunset for the men to go drinking. Working at the shop was usually long, but with Ader around, the sun seemed to be pinned in the sky with heavy duty glue. For the entire day, Ader rattled on and on (…and on) about the deal with Opete, about how the conversation would go at the drinking place and on and on. Winyo had drifted in and out of concentration like a drunken duck. By the evening she was so drained, she just wanted her mother to get the deal already. Unable to wait any longer, Ader had left her daughter to close up the shop and hurried on to the centre to wait for her husband there.

Winyo was in the process of closing up the shop and had just begun the task of bundling her things on the bicycle when a car pulled up. The car belonging to the Odyek family. Winyo paused wondering why they had come this late. The Odyeks mostly did their shopping in the morning. When only Guma alighted from the car, Winyo panicked.

In a flurry of motion, she rushed through the bolts of the shop door quickly to get them closed. The rusty metal protested like an annoyed wife, squealing and screeching as she worked the handle, further making her haste way too obvious.

"Could you not lock up?" came the familiar voice from behind her. Her heart skittered and launched into a pace so fast it had her head spinning. Closing her eyes, she inhaled slowly, attempting to calm her nerves. Good lord what was wrong with her! She needed to act normal.

"Winyo," he spoke again, his calm voice only flustering her more.

"I was just leaving," she spoke to the door.

"I have to buy something."

Of course, Winyo thought, why else would he be here? "I-I am locking up," she muttered as she furiously worked at the bolt which only wailed louder and refused to move.

He put his hand on her shoulder and slowly turned her round. His gentle touch sent languid warmth spreading through her like liquid silk, slipping and coiling in her tummy like a furry animal. He was too close, she thought dazedly as his scent hit her like a drug, sultry pine and wood.

Winyo's eyes drifted down to her feet, more to hide her embarrassing attraction to him than shyness. It was then that she noticed that the slippers she wore were torn with hideous dark mend patches of the strings, a signature of her father's recent recovery stitch work. Her feet were brown and caked with dust. Good lord.

"Are you okay?" he asked softly. "Do I frighten you?"

"No," Winyo said quickly before she shook her head and sighed in resignation, who was she kidding? "Yes, a little," she admitted. But he had not asked the question for the reasons that she responded to. He stiffened slightly, and Winyo wished she could take her words back, but she also was not going to correct him and confess that she was madly attracted to him.

His expression was carefully blank as he asked, "Do you believe that I will curse you?"

He was asking about the village rumours. Winyo's gaze drifted back to her feet. Gosh, was that her toe? She studied the big toe on her left foot: the nail was overgrown that it was splitting at the end and lined with dirt on the inside, so it was almost black. Actually, all her toenails were dirty. She needed to work on them. Acholla always had the best-looking feet, Winyo thought as she hoped her silence would prompt him to ask another question. It often worked like a charm; most people hated silence and liked to fill it with mundane stuff. Winyo's gaze drifted to his feet. He wore nice shoes, black leather, the kind that must have cost a lot of money. Winyo sighed, as she drew her eyes to her slipper clad feet. His elegant high and mighty dressing was making her excessively conscious of her thin old brown dress that had a few threads loose at the sides. Her hands slowly drifted to cover up the opening in her dress. His eyes followed her movement. She pressed herself onto the metal door behind.

He was clearly waiting for an answer, proving that he was the kind that was okay with silence.

"I don't know," she said finally in answer to his question.

Something akin to disappointment crossed his features before he blanked his expression and shrugged. "I just need to buy some more millet flour from you, nothing more."

"I am leaving."

"I find myself growing bored with this game, your attempt at flirtation is drab, unexciting and amateurish at best. I am here to shop, I will be spending a staggering amount of money, worth more than a week of sitting around in this miserable hole of a shop," he clipped harshly, "so open that door and give me what I want; then I can give you the money. Isn't that all that you people care about?"

Winyo's head reared back; it was almost like he had slapped her. The way he said *'You people'* like they were a venereal disease. *Had he heard some rumour about her mother?* He probably had. Her mother had more like a reputation, money was indeed all that Ader cared about and she made no secret of it, going by the number of village fights she involved herself in with debtors. Didn't mean that Winyo liked to have it thrown at her face like that or be called drab. She knew that she was not the prettiest flower in the field let alone the most exciting, but drab? Winyo quickly discovered that his lacking opinion of her hurt more that it should have.

She rapidly blinked back the sudden sting of tears at the back of her eyes. Ashamed beyond words to realize that she had been harbouring a desire that he would at least take some remote interest in her. Goodness, she was truly hopeless! What was it about her that guys found so unappealing? Was it her shyness? She pondered wearily.

Winyo sighed in resignation. "What do you want to buy?"

A tight polite smile slid across his face as he dug a piece of paper from his pocket and smoothly rattled off the list of things he needed, his voice smooth and sure and commanding. His purchase totaled up an amount that would certainly have her mother swooning.

"Wow, how can anyone say no to that," she said, hoping for a casual tone, but the awkwardness and tension sat in the air like a big fat hippopotamus.

His lips curled up into another non-smile and he said, "You don't."

"The rudeness was unnecessary," Winyo found herself muttering under her breath, but he heard her and stepped even closer.

"I was simply making statement of my observations."

"Well, they are wrong," Winyo said. He was way too close. His deep tantalizing, male scent engulfed her and blanketed her senses like a fog, her eyes nearly drifting, closed. Her heart was drumming way too loudly it was a mystery that he didn't hear it.

"Which part did I get wrong?" he murmured in her ear. Good glory, he was speaking in her ears! A shiver ran through her at the warm caress of his breath.

"I was not flirting," she whispered. Her voice had grown husky and she had to clear her throat.

"Weren't you?" His voice was low and hoarse as he said, "Why not?"

She didn't know what to say, did he want her to flirt with him? Or was he just looking for clarity? Was he flirting with her? Her mind was racing too fast and her mouth had gone entirely too dry.

"Tell me why you were watching me."

Her eyes flew to his, and the intensity in those dark brown eyes had her stomach clenching. She licked her dry lips and his eyes immediately traced the movement, heat banked up in his gaze. It was getting increasingly hard to breath. He made her body malfunction in an entirely delicious way.

"I shouldn't have done that," she spoke in answer. "That was a mistake."

He stiffened again at her words and took a step back. Winyo nearly protested at the loss of the unexpected intimacy; she wanted to yank him back and tell him that she meant to say that she should not have interrupted his privacy, but that would have been the height of desperation.

"Tell me, do you follow everybody around? Do you follow my brothers too? Or is it just me?"

"No, I don't—"

"...because if that were indeed the case, I would be happy to inform you of my next location in case you got the urge to...*watch me*?"

He did think that she was desperate and a loose skirt, Winyo thought as she studied the hint of amusement in his eyes. Disappointment sunk into her gut like a rusty, old metal ball. She then decided that this encounter had gone on far longer than was necessary. Turning to the shop door, she began fidgeting with the keys in her hand.

"I don't like watching you," she grumbled.

"Oh, I believe you." He placed his hand over his heart in mock agreement.

Winyo found her anger as she turned to face him. "You are enjoying yourself."

"Not yet, perhaps after we discuss the numerous places where you can have unlimited access to me, we could both have something to enjoy."

Winyo really couldn't tell if he was flirting or being a jerk. She wanted to find out more, but she noticed the children returning home after a long day of play, running down the road. Winyo backed away. She didn't want to be another story for them to take home.

"So, about the flour," Guma was saying, "Could you open the shop, right now?"

"You don't give me orders," she snapped, but he was not looking at her face anymore. His eyes rolled over her figure with excruciating slowness and lingered at the torn gap at the side of her dress that exposed a huge chunk of skin on her right side. She quickly ran her hands to her side, clutching the fabric together. She was wearing one of her more worn-out dresses. Darn it! Winyo almost laughed now. To think that she had actually entertained thoughts of his interest in her! Hilarious! He was definitely the kind of guy who had girls falling for him, girls with more than three dresses to their names and not as poor as she was with a mother who beat up anyone in debt to her.

"You are not supposed to stare," she said consciously, wishing the ground would open up and swallow her.

He deliberately stepped into her personal space again. "Little bird, I look wherever I want."

"I didn't tell you to look at me."

"Do I need permission to look at you?" he asked gently, a twinkle in his eye.

"It is bad manners," she said prudishly.

"Now you know all about manners," he scoffed. Winyo was about to answer back, but he was already on to something else. "Tell me, how many clothes do you have?"

"What?" she snapped, caught off guard.

"How many?"

"Why? Such impertinence. What gives you the right t–"

"Well, it's just that everytime I see you, you always have that dress on," he cut in smoothly, "It got me wondering if this is the only one you own."

She was mortified. If she ever wondered whether she had a chance with him, she was now sure that ship had sailed a long, long time ago.

"Is this the only dress you have, little bird?" he asked gently.

Her embarrassment had her looking away. "Everytime *you* see me? How many times have you seen me around?"

His smiled came easy. "A lot."

"No, wrong answer," she snapped angrily, struggling to hold back the tears stinging the back of her eyes. "You –you have not seen me enough to be able to judge the clothes that I wear."

"I was just–"

"Trying to insult me. Who do you think you are? Just–just because you have a fancy car and fancy shoes, you think you can criticize the way I dress?!"

"I wasn't doing that," he said quickly. She could tell he was trying to calm her down – well, she was having none of that.

"Listen, it's just that you are always wearing that dress and it has such a terrible color."

"Terrible color?!"

"Look little bird, you are taking this the wrong way."

What other way was she supposed to take it? "Are you saying that I am stupid?!"

"No, that's not it either. What is wrong with you, woman?" he raised his voice in exasperation. "Well, if you must know, no one should dress like that in daylight–let alone every day."

Her back stiffened at the insult and she watched the remorse drench his face as he realized the depth of his words. He looked like he was about to say something, but Winyo gave him her back to him and once more continued with her inglorious attempt at unbolting the door. Surely, was there no end to her humiliation?

The hand he placed on top of hers was hesitant but gentle. Its soothing warmth did the miracle of quelling down some of her hurt and embarrassment.

"We have guests coming," he spoke quietly, "None of my brothers may be able to come here tomorrow. That's why I insist on purchasing the flour today."

"Guests?" she asked curiously as she looked at him over her shoulder. However, her question seemed to irritate him, judging by the frown that creased his forehead.

"Don't look so surprised," he spat, snatching his hands away from her. "We do get guests."

She did not want to pursue that. Without a word, she opened the door and was measuring his items. He was angry she could tell, but heck! So was she. Maybe it was one of those upside down days because neither of them seemed to be able to get appropriate words to say to one another without hurting the other.

She finished his order and Guma helped her close the door. The bolt easily slid through his hands like it too knew that they both needed to get away.

"Thank you," he said tightly, and then he was back into the car and driving off.

It was after the car had disappeared from view that she looked down at her clothes. The son of Alice Odyek was right about one thing, her poverty was beginning to show. And she hated that it had been the only notable thing that had stood out about her.

She needed new clothes.

3

"Has your uncle done anything about his wife's behaviour yet?" Acholla asked. It was early in the afternoon and the sun was unrelenting. It was their fifth and last trip to the borehole for the day. Winyo's neck felt strained as she balanced the heavy jerrycan of water on her head. Acholla looked like she was struggling with her load too. The last water trip was always the hardest.

"Atang can do whatever she likes," Winyo replied distantly.

"What time did she come home last night?"

"Late," she replied curtly.

"What story did she come up with?"

"I don't know, I wasn't listening much."

Acholla stopped in her track. Winyo's attention veered back to Acholla.

"Winyo, are you okay?"

"I am fine, why?" she answered, puzzled.

"It is just that you have barely spoken since morning, and every time you do, it is with a one-line responses. Have I done something to annoy you?"

Winyo glanced down the main path into the footpath which meandered its way into the bush like an old drunk all the way to a valley where stood the village borehole, noisy and always filled with people. She couldn't remember a single person that she spoke to at the borehole today. Her thoughts had been occupied; Acholla's words had flown by her like dust in the wind. To Acholla she said, "Nothing is wrong, I just don't feel like talking."

"You should have told me that instead of making me talk with myself all day."

"Is this dress really that bad?" she interrupted. She hadn't been able to shake off the misery at being scrutinized and found lacking by Guma. This in turn had her wondering if that was the reason that none of the guys in the village ever took interest in her.

Acholla looked her over then shook her head. "No, why do you ask?"

"No particular reason."

"Anyway, we were told not to stay out long after dark," Acholla said as they resumed their careful trek home. "They say a lion escaped from Kidepo national park. So, avoid any late trips if you can."

Winyo wished Acholla hadn't made that particular revelation, for, it all came back to her later that day when she was riding her bicycle alone in the dark after another late rice delivery. Winyo's mother had sent her to Kitgum Matidi to deliver flour and rice. It had been sometime in the afternoon after her return from the borehole, and the both of them had known it was a bad idea. She was sure to get back home late. As usual, Ader ignored this and ordered her to ride extra fast.

So, she had clambered on to the bicycle and ridden to Kitgum Matidi. Her Uncle Saul was there and by the looks of it, he must have already been there before her arrival, but it had not been to him that she had been sent. Ader had sent her to an old customer's shop in Kitgum Matidi centre; it was after making the delivery that she had been delayed. Uncle Saul had been at the front of the small shop, man spread over a woven seat. The sight of him always sent bile churning in her belly like a witch's pot.

He was her mother's brother and as sleazy as a lizard. Her mother had five brothers and two sisters. Her aunties were married to men who lived very far away, and her other uncles had gone to Sudan where they were carrying out trade, but not Uncle Saul. He stayed. Tonight, he had insisted she stay on a while and held her up with questions about her family and how the shop was doing. He had been the cause of her delay at Kitgum Matidi.

She hated the times when she met him on her way to some of the villages. On several occasions she had run away from him when she was sure he had not noticed her presence.

Winyo wished he had gone to Sudan; at least that way she wouldn't have to deal with him. Occasionally when he came home, he always insisted that Winyo attend to him and the way he looked at her– well it was no way an uncle should look at a niece. It was way too thorough and appraising; he reminded her of the greedy way Okeny always drooled over her body. No, he was worse that Okeny, because Okeny did not think that he had ownership of her. Uncle Saul thought being related to her meant he had some sorts of rights over her, which Winyo never understood at all.

At first she had doubted her observation of the situation, refusing to believe that her uncle would look at her as a woman– but judging from the recent visit, and the way his hands had trailed to her slender thighs as she bent to serve him food or water, there was nothing chaste there.

She had noted with growing resentment at how his hands lingered on the small of her back as he guided her through a door. His hands kept on getting increasingly bolder, for now he had no issue spanking her butt playfully as she walked by; the rest of the family laughed it off as the joke he made it to be, but Winyo knew better now. During his visits, Winyo had swallowed her discomfort and counted the days until he left. Unfortunately, the older she got the more his visits had increased.

She had considered mentioning this development to her mother but had ruled against it. Uncle Saul was her mother's best friend in the family. He was the one that she trusted the most, so in all honesty there was no way in a million years that Ader would believe her version of the situation. It was not like he had said anything inappropriate. But actions spoke louder than words, right?

Today, she had not been quick enough to get away from him. He had delayed her in Kitgum Matidi. Winyo regretted the delay because nighttime had found her still on the road, a long way from home. It got too dangerous to ride and Acholla's words about a lion on the roam generously poisoned her. The moon was high and the road deserted. Only the rhythmic metal sounds emitting from the bicycle occupied the otherwise deathly quiet of the road as she pedaled back home.

The road was wide and it shone white against the moonlight. It was the same road that ran all the way past their shop in the village and the village centre, then all the way to Sudan. It was still a long ride home.

Winyo had convinced herself that she would ride all the way home, but thoughts of thieves and roaming lions got the better of her. She had to stop and taken refuge under the shelter of a tree. This, of course, had her traumatized with thoughts of snakes and gigantic spiders – she stayed awake for nearly the entire night.

Her mother was furious the next day.

Winyo's arrival home had been the first sight that greeted Ader when she opened the door in the morning. She had yelled on and on about what a fool of a daughter she had. After that, the yelling turned into demands of where she had spent the night–with which man in particular.

In the heat of rage Ader had given her a thorough beating and there after demanded that her father do the same. Ader had then declared that she was never going to leave her daughter alone, even for one second of the day. She then took it upon herself to go with Winyo to the shop that day which she really didn't have to.

Just when she had thought her day wouldn't get any worse, it did. The large silver range rover, belonging to none other than the Odyek family pulled up in front of their shop– at the precise moment that her mother had launched into another of her verbal attacks. Yes, Ader had since morning been taking breaks in between the insults that she dished out with traumatizing efficiency, and she had just revitalized her word library when Guma stepped out of the car. The last thing Winyo wanted was to have her mother insult her in his presence.

Guma was alone, none of his brothers were with him. He was a sight to behold - dark hair, perfect face, strong, lean, muscular build that showed through the thin white shirt he wore, matched with dark pants that hugged him like a glove. Her heart broke at the beauty that was wrapped up in one unattainable package. He was like the last ripe mango at the top of the tree that nobody would ever reach.

Her mother had quieted down by the time Guma was within ear shot- which was out of character, her mother usually rambled loudest when she had an audience but right now Winyo was grateful for her silence.

"Hello Guma," Winyo greeted gaily- far too gaily. Perhaps it was the drag of a terrible night and the tediousness of having to listen to her mother's ramblings that was taking a toll at her, but there she was, beaming up at Guma like he was the messiah. Goodness knows she needed rescuing– only her hero was not as excited to assume the role.

He scowled darkly down at her, and it took only a moment for her to realize that his mood was not very far off from what her mother was currently nursing.

"Five kilos rice and three kilos of maize cereal, please," he clipped, deliberately avoiding a proper greeting.

Winyo didn't have the good sense to feel insulted. For once she actively tried to keep him around longer- anything to give her a break from her mother. For some reason, Ader had piped down in his presence and she was not willing to lose this magical goose yet. To Guma, she brightly said, "Is that all you are getting, for today? I must say, you are getting slow on me. What is it that you were telling me about having lots of guests?"

His eyes slowly narrowed at her in surprised suspicion. "I don't keep records of every conversation that I have with you."

Winyo felt her smile falter, but she soldiered on. "So, who were the visitors that you entertained last time?"

"That is none of your business," he said curtly. This time her smile wobbled and finally dropped as her heart chilled with the frost in his tone. This was just not her day. She quickly bent over to complete his order; for a second there, she caught her mother's eye, something she wished she hadn't done. Ader looked like she was at the verge of raining knives upon her head.

"My mother is not feeling well," Guma spoke then, taking her by surprise. Was he extending an olive branch? Winyo waited but he appeared to have spoken all he had to say.

"Well, I hope she feels better soon," Winyo said, though she really didn't know Alice Odyek at all.

"Thanks, Winyo," he said. He looked like he was searching for more words to say. Winyo opened her mouth to say more but snapped it shut. She always seemed to say the wrong words to him. The awkward silence stretched on forever before Winyo decided to hand him his order.

Ader had all the while been making a show of looking into the records. Just as he turned to leave, Winyo felt her mother move close to her side and, being the daughter she had been to her mother for twenty long years, she knew that the flow of words were inevitable.

Ader had taken a long enough break with the arrival of Guma. She probably was eager to start where she had left off.

"What is she sick of?" Winyo found herself calling after Guma. She was going to hell, using others to keep her punishment at bay. In all honesty, she wondered why her mother would think she, Winyo, would like to sleep at the side of the road, in the middle of nowhere. No, wait, her mother's version was of her spending a night at her 'lover's' house. *Sigh.*

"Slight case of Malaria, just when we have a wedding to organise. It is really going to be hard, she knows a lot more about these things than we do," Guma said in a rush of words. "It is all quite overwhelming, considering that not many people are willing to help us. I don't even understand why my uncle wants us involved in the wedding at all. We would only cause more harm than good."

Her heart tightened at the admission of a vulnerability that she was surprised he revealed to her. So, the village rumours did bother him after all. He was always so stoic she thought he didn't care. His eyes bore into hers as if he needed something from her. She wanted to give him a hug, but she was not sure how he would take that, or her mother, for that matter.

"There is a lot to a wedding, but you can handle it. I am sure there are people who can help you with it," Winyo added, frantically trying to think of who would dare step into the Odyek compound.

He paused at the door of the car. "Winyo, do you know anything about traditional weddings?"

"Who– me? I–" she stuttered.

"Yes, she does!" Ader pipped up like a lark. Winyo took that instance of mortified surprise to stare directly upon her mother's face.

"She has been attending weddings since she could walk," Ader continued with her unwanted revelations as she slapped Winyo on the back like she was her favorite child. "I am sure she knows what to do

51

when it comes to the preparation, don't you Winyo?"

Was this a trick question? "Emmhh, I ...I –"

"You see, she knows," Ader made a joyous confirmation of something that Winyo was not even sure about; she knew where her mother was going with this.

"That is nice," Guma said with relief spreading across his face.

"I am sure if you need any help, she would be more than willing to help, and she could get a ton of people to come too," Ader called at Guma.

"Really?" They both chorused at the same time.

"Yes," Ader sang. "Tell him Winyo." She nudged her with an elbow. Winyo blinked; apparently, she was supposed to agree with this and offer some sort of speech presentation.

The last thing she wanted was to arrange a wedding, something that she had no experience with despite her mother's feigned positivity. If there was anyone who knew about such things it was none other than Ader herself.

"Can you help with the arrangements?" Guma asked her, rather too hopefully, Winyo painfully noted.

"I think," she replied lengthily.

"She will come to your house soon enough to help out," Ader announced. Winyo stared at her.

Guma ran his hands through his hair as relief seemed to wash over him. "Thanks a lot. It had been such a worry in my mind. We are our uncle's only close family as you know, and I didn't want him to not have a great wedding because of us."

"I understand, everyone deserves a great wedding," Ader said, nodding with empathy etched over every feature on her face, it was almost comical, "And we are all about the helping, aren't we?" The question was directed to Winyo, who nodded dumbly. The absurdity of the situation was hilarious. Winyo ran a hand across her face to brush off the smile that threatened the corner of her lips. Her mother, who could not stand the thought of her daughter speaking with the Odyek sons was pronouncing herself village Samaritan and friend to the Odyek family. Not to mention throwing that same daughter she had been warning right into their house.

"Wow, now I am so glad I came here today," Guma was saying, "So, when should we expect you?" The question was directed at Winyo and once again she was at a loss of words, an asset that Ader always had in full arsenal.

"How about tomorrow?" Ader answered.

"That would be perfect. Thanks a lot, Winyo," he said. "I'll see you tomorrow then." Winyo nodded, wondering if he really had not noticed that it was her mother who had done most of the talking.

For a while they stared in silence as the car took a corner and disappeared into the distance. Once again Winyo was left alone with her mother. It was hard to judge her mood– it was hard to judge her *own* mood.

All day she had been resigned to silence and listening to her mother's insults but now what she felt was an unbalanced mixture of fury and fear of what her mother's reaction would be like if she were to decline helping the Odyeks, based on the fact that she did not know the first or last thing about traditional weddings. The whole spending the night away from home thing was still hanging in the air like like fresh dung.

"Mama, I don't know anything about weddings," Winyo began carefully. It didn't take a genius to realize that the whole point of this new kindness to the Odyeks was so that they could get an opportunity to supply the needed items for the wedding.

"There is nothing hard about it. I will talk you through it. This is a perfect opportunity for us- we need this," Ader said as she flipped through the records. "You will go to Alice, first thing tomorrow, and talk to her real nice and make her see the kind of good people we are."

"She is a witch, you said so yourself."

"Who cares?" Ader burst out, "They will be buying half of what we have in the shop if not everything. That means a lot of money for us."

"But–"

"Winyo, if it means trading my entire shop to the devil for that kind of money, I will gladly do that," Ader snapped crossly, effectively shutting down any more protest. "Anyway, Alice can't do anything to you."

"You are sure?"

"Of course, I am sure," Ader said in exaggerated exasperation. "You are going to be helping them, I am sure even a witch has the decency to be grateful."

"I don't know how to organize a traditional wedding," she insisted. The very thought terrified her. She was not good with people. She was way too shy for that. A traditional wedding involved bringing relatives together, sending messages back and forth between the two involved families. It needed experience in discussions about bride price and dowry. It simply needed a loose convincing tongue like Ader's, not Winyo.

"And what a perfect chance for you to learn," Ader crowed dismissively. Clearly that conversation with Guma had made her day and Ader suddenly seemed to be in a much better mood than she had this morning.

Her mood as dark as a charred pot, Winyo furiously set onto the unnecessary task of sorting the beans into small bags. She sometimes wished she had the courage to stand up to her mother, but Ader was so intimidating and talked way too fast it was hard to even get a word in during an argument. Not that she ever argued with her. She always agreed with and did everything that her mother demanded. If she didn't like it, she sulked until she got over it. Ader could easily whip her into submission, so she quickly discovered that it was much easier to tuck her head in.

Winyo found herself wondering as she often did, of how much different her life would be if she got married and had her own home. She would no longer be under the controlling thumb of Ader. Most girls her age were married with children of their own, but Winyo and a few of her friends who had chosen to keep studying were among the unmarried girls. She knew for a fact that the parents of the twins already had selected suitors for them to marry as soon as they finished school. A lot of the weddings in the village were organized, especially for the young girls who had so many suitors vying for their hand. Her mother had not once come up with a suitor suggestion, so Winyo assumed that she was being left to find her own partner, like most unpopular girls.

Most of the eligible guys in the village were not interested in her anyway. Though her pickings were limited, she certainly did not want to end up a spinster. She had observed how the spinsters in the village were treated. Well, they were treated the way Ader treated her now, like a child whose opinion didn't matter. They were shunned and as a result they banded together. Winyo shuddered at the thought of one day joining that group.

Thoughts of marriage had her thinking of Guma Odyek. He obviously was way out of her league, but she couldn't help but wonder what it would be like to be his partner. She already knew he was a patient listener, but was he a caring partner? A generous friend and an attentive lover? Acholla's mother had said those were the qualities of a good husband. Winyo shook her head at the thoughts that whirled in her mind. It was a shame he found her lacking.

"I will be going to the center now," Ader announced.

Winyo realized that she had been right in her previous analysis, Ader was indeed in a better mood.

"Tend to the shop as good as I would," her mother instructed as she busied herself, straightening her dress and dusting herself here and there. "Ensure that you sleep at home tonight, so you better be there before I get there."

She was out of the shop before Winyo could answer–not that she had anything to say. Her mother was clearly in a rush to get out of there.

Working on a wild guess, Winyo could bet that she was going to look for her gossip buddy, Aketo, the short, plump woman who sold smoked fish at the market. Beside her mother, Aketo and her group of friends at the market were the loudest women that she knew of. There was no gossip that did not pass by them– it usually passed *through* them.

Winyo sighed wearily as she ran her hands through her hair. Her options were between organizing the wedding or starting her own home.

4

Uncle Saul.

Her most recent meeting with him had left her feeling so sickened with the entire male population that she had refused to speak with her brothers for an entire day.

Today presented new problems for her. It had been late in the morning, and she had been tending to the shop when her mother had sent the twins Acen and Apio for her. Turns out a messenger had arrived from Agoro, her mother's village. Uncle Saul had made an order for a sack of millet cereal and requested (more like demanded) that she, Winyo, deliver the order herself. He had the gull to insist that if his 'favorite' niece didn't make the delivery, he wouldn't pay for it. *The jerk.*

So, there she was, standing in the middle of her home compound, having an argument (one she knew she wouldn't win) with her mother. Ader was working on the grinding stone beside the kitchen hut, grinding groundnuts into paste for lunch. Winyo stood in the middle of the compound, rocking the baby in her arms.

"You said it yourself. I have to go to the Odyek home today- you got me into this. I can't go to Agoro today," Winyo argued out her case.

"If it means that by evening we shall be having more money than we did this morning, then you will crawl to Lake Victoria if I tell you to."

"Mama, I can't go, Guma must be waiting for–"

"Winyo, the wedding is not going to happen anytime soon. The Odyeks can wait, what is your problem?" Ader was running out of patience.

"Can't one of the boys go?" she asked, referring to one of her brothers who were lazing about under a tree, eating fruits.

Ader paused midway, from her chore to stare at her daughter incredulously, her paste marred hands travelled to her hips, an action she usually did when she was provoked. The fact that she barely noticed the mess that her hands caused to her dress was testament enough to her anger. Winyo didn't have to hear the rest of her words to know that she was going to Agoro.

"Winyo," Ader began as she visibly and deeply inhaled for patience, "your brothers have things to do at home. The least you can do is visit a relative who is going to pay for what we should be giving – for free!!" She was just getting started. "What kind of a child are you?! We are supposed to care about our relatives. No one is a mountain, or an island, whatever it is that people say. Are you an island? Winyo, answer me!!" Ader didn't wait for a reply. "I tell you to go to your uncle, you act like it is a punishment– as if it is a punishment to visit my relatives! Saul is my brother, Winyo are you listening to this?" Ader had put her hand to her own ear in the sign language of asking her if she was listening. "You don't want to see my brother, as if there is something wrong with your mother's family– is there something wrong with me? Winyo?!"

"No, mama."

"Tell me why it is, again, that you don't want to go to Agoro. Repeat it loud and clear, I want to hear it!"

Winyo wished the ground would swallow her. "Nothing, I – I was just worried about a promise that I made to Guma. I – I am sure it is not important–"

"Of course, it is important," Ader snapped at her like she was an idiot. "That is why on your way, you shall pass by the Odyek home and inform them of the situation and tell them that your mother will come by in the evening to help in your stead."

"Okay." It was weird, to think that she had not wanted to go to the Odyek home in the first place. Now it was like the one thing that she would rather do.

Her heart was heavy as she rode out of their home compound on her trusty bicycle. Her luck wasn't at its best. Her worries were numerous. Taking a long journey at this time of the day was unthinkable; there was no way in hell's luck that she would make it to Agoro and back before dark. High chances were that she would make it *there* by dark. *What was wrong with her mother?!* Winyo thought crossly. Ader had been lecturing her for days about how spending the night away for home was unacceptable.

Currently, her possibilities were between spending a night in Agoro– with her uncle and spending another night along the road side. Both those options made her want to claw her heart out with a rusty nail.

The sun was burning hot, a heat wave that always swept by before the rain. She raised her face to study the sky and as expected, dark clouds hung heavy in the sky above the horizon, floating like graceful elephants in a herd below the lingering white clouds but slowly drifting forward, sealing her doom. Her day was not getting any better.

The large compound at the Odyek residence was deserted. Winyo stayed on her bicycle wondering what to do next, silently hoping someone would notice her presence. She was not ready to go inside the house, not today. Her stomach was twisted in such tight knots she worried that she would throw up.

Eventually someone came out. It was Okwera, Earnest was right behind him. Winyo fidgeted with the bicycle brakes as she waited for them, the load at the back of her bicycle was so heavy, she had to plant both of her feet on the ground to keep from tipping over. It was going to be a long ride to Agoro. For the thousandth time that day she found herself cursing Uncle Saul.

"Is that for us?" Okwera asked good-naturedly.

"I wish," she replied, "that way I wouldn't have to ride far away from home today."

"You are going somewhere?" Earnest asked puzzled. "Guma said you would be here with us, or did I get that wrong?"

"You didn't get anything wrong. My mother will be coming here sometime later in the afternoon. I have somewhere to go."

"Must you go?" Okwera asked, "We were all expecting you…"

"Anxiously," Earnest added with a grin. Winyo laughed at his easy humour.

"We received an urgent order and as it turns out, I am the only one that can make it there today," Winyo explained.

"You don't look too happy, are you okay?" Earnest asked. "Can we help?"

"I am not sad, just a bit upset." *Huge understatement.* "I only came to inform you that my mother will be here in my stead, and now I shall be off."

"Safe travels, we shall tell Guma that you came by," said Okwera. "He will be disappointed."

Winyo felt miserable, way too miserable to decipher that mind spin. She really needed to chill. Her heart was lodged somewhere between hell and the pit of her stomach. The only way she would feel calm was if she were on her way back home.

Alone again, riding the dusty path to Agoro under the unrelenting sun, the vast savanna spread out before her in alternating impressive shades of green and browns as the winds rustled their peace. The majestic mountains rose steadily before her like ancient gods, magnificently painting the horizon in dark blue and grey. Their ridges were more defined as one neared Agoro. All the mountains were named according to the villages that they were situated in. There was Got-Lamuo, Got-Seresenya, Got Madi, Got Agoro. The word 'Got' was an Acholli word for mountain.

Usually when she rode down the winding path towards their direction, the grandeur of the mountains always managed to lift up her spirits, and today was no exception. She raised her head to the sky and let the cold wind caress her face as she peddled down the road. She relaxed and allowed the sweet blend of nature and moisture drenched air to tranquilize her edgy senses. For a moment she forgot about what she was riding to – but only for a moment.

Evening found her at the foot of Got Madi, the mountain belonging to the village of Madi Opei. At least it was near Agoro. From there, though, it was another hour's ride to Agoro. Got Agoro was bigger than the Got Madi and it usually cast a shadow over Agoro village, meaning it already had to be dark in Agoro while she was basking in the light at Madi- Opei.

Throughout the ride, she had humoured herself that she could manage to make a quick return trip like most people that she knew of, but she was not most people and she was slow, always had been. She could power through the rest of the journey, but one thing was painfully certain: she was spending the night in Agoro, and most likely at Uncle Saul's house. Winyo decided then that she would rather spend the entire night riding back home than sleep at his house.

Uncle Saul lived in an iron roofed house. A very nice two bedroom bungalow house that was the envy of the village. He was a rich man according to the village standards, but certainly not as much as the Odyek family. Saul owned businesses in Kitgum town, which were well attended so that he could run his other trade businesses in Sudan from a base in Agoro.

When Winyo finally arrived, the bright lights at his house were turned on. His house was not one to be missed, especially in the night. Solar power panels blazed electric light from every side of the house, highlighting the house like a beacon in a village that mostly used lamps for light.

Right now, music drifted from the open windows as she wheeled her bicycle into the compound. The terrible feeling that she had been holding at bay returned with such vengeance that she contemplated just leaving her bundle at the front door and making a run for it. She looked at the sky and sighed. It looked like it would rain at night, and she didn't want the delivery damaged by water.

She glanced around the darkened village. Uncle Saul's house was secluded, and the nearest neighbor was indeed a good walk away. *Perhaps it would be better if she stayed the night at her friend Jackie's home,* Winyo contemplated. Jackie was one of the students that she studied with in Kitgum town. She had told Winyo that she lived in Agoro. The thought was starting to get an appeal in her mind when it occurred to her that she didn't know where Jackie's house was. And she was too exhausted to start searching around the village. Word would most certainly go around, and Uncle Saul would know that she shunned his house. Eventually her mother would find out, which surely meant she was a dead bird walking. She was going to have to knock at Uncle Saul's house, make the delivery and ride back home. She would convince her mother that she was taking her lectures to heart about spending the night at home. Winyo gauged that it would be dead of night before she returned home.

Taking in a long shaky breath, she swallowed a pill of courage and knocked on the gigantic metal door. She had just convinced herself to make a run for it when the sudden jumble of bolts rooted her to the ground. The door swung open, and there was Uncle Saul. His large form filling up the door, a toothy smile stretching across his dark chubby face, his large toad eyes nearly popping out of his head.

"Winyo!!" he hailed, moments before his beefy arms engulfed her in a tight sweaty hug, crushing her frail form against him. She struggled for breath.

"I thought you would not come," he spoke into her face, ruthlessly crowding her space.

"Mama said I had to come but I left home late," Winyo explained with strain, twisting her face away from him, all the while trying to ignore that the thick hands around her waist were beginning to take on a squeezing motion. Her stomach churned so violently she got bile in her mouth.

"Where is the millet?" he asked. Winyo hooked a thumb to the direction of the bicycle parked in the middle of the compound, his eyes followed her motion, seconds after he exclaimed, "All that sack for this tiny body of yours." He was now shaking her weak exhausted arms. "How do you manage?"

Like he hadn't asked for a full sack, she thought darkly as she tried to evade more groping. "I am used to it," she replied wearily.

"How about you come inside now, you must be tired, you poor Sweetie." He had now taken claim of her chin between two of his fat fingers. Winyo fixed her gaze onto the room behind him. It was taking all her might to clear the revulsion off her face.

"I will bring everything inside- you go inside, Sweetie," he said again, shoving her into the house but not without giving a loud vulgar slap on her bottom.

Winyo stumbled into the house and nearly lost her balance. There went her plan of making a quick exit.

The dining room was large. A long table occupied the middle of the room. Of the six chairs at the table, Saul had ensured that he sat on the one closest to her. Throughout dinner his hands kept drifting to her knees despite the number of times that she pushed them away.

Needless to say, dinner was a long and torturous ordeal. Winyo managed to choke down a few mouthfuls but could not recall what she ate nor what the conversation had been about. Her troubles however began after dinner.

Saul had shown her to her the room for the night, then he had taken her into the large clean kitchen and instructed her to clean up the dishes. Relaxing a little, she had assumed this was the end to her evening, then she would sneak out of the house and make a run for it. She had thought wrong.

Her back had been to the door, so she never saw him come back into the room. Her only warning had been the pungent smell of male sweat before giant arms locked her in a tight hold. She gasped in shocked terror as she tried to turn around, but her arms were trapped. Fear rose before her mind's eye like an enraged phantom.

"What are you doing?!" she shrieked in alarm.

"Come now, my dear, come now - we both know you want it," he growled low into her ears, "You have been teasing me for months now. Today we get to do something about it…"

"Let me go! Now!" She wildly wriggled and struggled to free her imprisoned arms but her muscles were exhausted from the long day's ride and his strength was far superior to hers. Heavens help her, she was alone with him! The nearest house was a good few meters away. No one would hear her screams.

"Winyo," came the hoarse voice from behind her as he ground his hard arousal against her back. There was no mistaking his intentions. Panic shot through her system like an incensed lightning bolt. She had to get away!

"Noooo!!" she screamed, pushing away from the sink in a struggle to extricate herself from the dirty incestuous hold.

"I have waited so very long for this moment, darling," he grunted into her hair as he groped at her breasts. She wanted to claw his eyes out- her hands were trapped, he held them firmly in front of her. She screamed out in frustration.

"Stop this right now –I –I will tell Mama!!"

"She won't believe you," he assured her, as he obscenely ground against her again and groaned in obvious pleasure. She screamed out again, this time with blinding revulsion. She fought harder, doubling her effort but the adrenaline spike was providing more terror than energy.

"Get away from me!" she screamed. He was not listening. The vile harsh breathing at the back of her neck sent bile into her lungs. She tried to tackle with the force of her shoulders but that had him bending her over which was not a good position for her.

"Winyo, stop this now!" He sounded angry now as she continued her struggle.

Winyo fought harder. She would be damned if she stopped resisting him. She broke skin as she bit hard into his arm. He cursed and let go of her. She kicked and thrashed out of his hold, but he easily kicked her feet off the ground, the wind rushing out of her lungs as she crashed on the floor.

Then he was hitting her, his fist slamming into her face so hard, nearly knocking her out. He barked at her to stop fighting him, which she didn't listen. He slammed another blow to the side of her head and this time she blacked out.

When Winyo woke up, she was in a dark room. A gag covered her mouth, her hands bound to her feet. It was already morning. Images of last night jolted her into reality. She was still in Uncle Saul's house.

That bastard!

She struggled to get free, but the ropes were firm and she could barely get up. When Uncle Saul finally came into the room, Winyo thought she would die from thirst and exhaustion. Her muscles were so cramped up that her breath had become laboured.

He stood over her like a mountain in the gloom. "Are you ready to give me what I want, Winyo?" he asked. "Or are you going to keep on pretending that you don't want this too. I have seen the way you look at me."

Winyo shot him a glare that would have felled an army. He was mad, he truly was mad, Winyo thought as she took stock of her situation.

"I have endured enough teasing from you. It's time to give me what you always torture me with, that sweet, delectable body," he said as he licked his dark sausage lips.

Cold sweat broke against her skin and she now began trembling in earnest as the realization finally sank in. There was only one way that she was leaving this place.

As his whore.

Tears flooded her eyes as she tried to plead with him through the gag. He reached out for her, and she hastily tried to shuffle away, kicking and screaming a muffled, "No," her eyes helplessly pleading for him to let her go. All the while common sense screaming at her that only a miracle would save her from this lunatic. It was this that drove her into a mindless kick frenzy.

Uncle Saul didn't try too hard to force her cooperation; after trying to still her kicking legs, he tied her legs back up again. "Looks like we are still playing hard to get, ehhh, Sweetie?' he said, "I intend to enjoy myself when we finally do this, Winyo, and we will do this. I will come back later."

Then he had gone. He did not come back again. Winyo couldn't remember a time that she had ever been this terrified. All day her mind kept going back and forth between what Uncle Saul was going to do to her and what her mother was thinking about her right now. The woman probably thought she had gone off somewhere with one of her 'many' lovers. She couldn't, for the life of her, fathom why her mother would think this? Everybody at home knew that she was painfully shy, and besides Okeny, no guy in the village had shown even remote interest in her.

Could it be that she enticed and flirted with men without even realizing it? Winyo wondered. She had trivial small talks with Uncle Saul and she barely spoke with Guma, yet Guma thought she had been flirting with him. Now her uncle claimed that she had been teasing him. Did she send out some sort of sexual whore vibe without even realizing it? Winyo racked her mind. Was this why males avoided her like the plague?

Winyo laid there desperately hoping that the ropes would somehow melt and she would run home and never see Uncle Saul again.

Uncle Saul did come back. It was later in the night. Winyo couldn't tell what time of night it was. Somehow, she had fallen asleep and woken up with a start at the large fingers that ran all over her. Groping and squeezing. Harsh breathing on her skin and his foul scent, thick as smoke coated the back of her throat, choking her with revulsion.

She tried to scream, but like air in a drum, the gag kept her voice at the back of her throat. Tears of desperation filled her eyes as she struggled against him. It was useless. She had not eaten all day and she was starved and weak. Squirming and kicking like an up turned bug, she fought but she was no match for him, despite her best efforts.

Somehow the clothes were off, and he was on top of her. He had freed her legs but had kept her hands bound. At some point she did recall giving up the fight for there was nothing to fight for anymore. Her honor was taken, her virginity stolen. Her innocence, gone.

All the while she laid there, crying as her mother's brother used her.

After he was done, he left her there. She spent the rest of the night on the floor, crying her soul out, her heart black as the night that blanketed her cursed day.

The next day he let her go.

5

They were angry.

Her mother and father were in the home compound on the morning she arrived. They were mad, yes, they were. It took Winyo a while to register that they were yelling at her. Her mind was a puff of cotton, floating somewhere outside her body which felt so numb, and her heart hurt so badly that tears failed her. She had cried herself into a husk the night before.

They were all in the compound, her mother, her brothers, her father with his brother, even Atang was there. They were mad at her for spending nights away from home. Some of the neighbors were coming to listen in to the commotion taking place at their compound.

Winyo had tried to explain but no one was listening to her. They just refused to listen. Even when she answered their questions, they did not believe her. Her clothes were torn, her parents needed an explanation for that as well. She felt even more humiliated than she had the night before as she tried to explain that she had been raped, right there in the presence of the entire gathered crowd. Her parents had taken the tiniest bit from her explanation and demanded that she reveal the man that she was having an affair with. To this most of the older women had demanded to know if he was a married man.

When her replies were less than satisfactory, a stick was brought out and the entire world was there to witness her humiliation as her parents whipped her before the crowd that had gathered.

The treacherous tears came then, hot and marred with guilt and shame that no water could wash off. Some of the older men jeered at her, the older women were even less sympathetic.

Winyo sank down in the dust and wept while accusations rained down upon her. Her mother was thoroughly disappointed in her and her father said that he was ashamed of her. Still the earth refused to swallow her.

Finally, she was sent to her hut. The one place that she had wanted to go to ever since she got back home. She needed to hide. Life had no meaning anymore.

"Where have you been?"

Winyo looked up blankly, and her gaze zeroed on Guma who sat perched on a rock at the side of the road. Winyo was on her way to the borehole. She hadn't noticed Guma on the way. He was holding one of his books and a pencil was tucked behind his ears.

"What?" Winyo asked.

"I haven't seen you in a while." He hopped off the rock. "The last time we met, you were in such a commendable mood and offered to help with our family affairs. I haven't seen you since then."

"Oh, I am sorry," she said, though sorry was the last thing that she felt for anyone but herself. "Didn't your brothers tell you? That my mother would be doing all the –er- necessary things."

"They told me," he agreed. "As for your mother, I have seen a lot of her and way too often, I should add, with the risk of sounding offensive."

"I am not offended."

"So?"

"So, what?"

He chuckled. "Where have you been? You seem so distracted, what is it? You have passed by me three times today and would have done so again if I hadn't made my presence known."

"No, that's not true, I would have seen you."

"Nope, you have been trotting with your head down like a grazing donkey, the few times that your eyes looked my way, you stared straight through me."

"A grazing donkey?"

"Again– no offence, my mouth seems to be where my eyes are today...I am an artist..." he stuttered. Winyo shook her head; her thought process was extra slow. It had been two weeks since her encounter with Uncle Saul and somedays she floated about in such a numb state that she barely registered her surroundings. Most of the times during the day she tried to blank out the pain, but somehow the terror and humiliation and feeling of loss always managed to rear their ugly heads and drag her down. At night, enduring the nightmares wrecked her soul, her torment seemed unending.

Guma strolled back to the seat that he had been occupying and came back flipping through a large sketch pad with the intention of showing her something. Winyo forced her attention to the dark pencil drawings. Soon enough the images of grazing animals came to her recognition-donkeys to be more precise. All done with clever, gentle but deliberate strokes of the pencil; she could almost feel their movement ooze out of the paper.

"You are really good at this," she had to admit as she took the book from him. "Where are they?"

"What? The donkey, it was grazing here earlier, I am sure you have seen it before, it belongs to Odoch at the village not very far from here." When she kept staring at him questioningly, he added, "It is just one donkey but drawn in all different poses."

"Clever," she said.

"You like it?" he stated as he took the book from her. "Would you like me to give it to you? Heck, I want to give it to you," he added as he ripped the page from his book and handed it to her.

Winyo looked at it and didn't know what to say. He was actually engaging in a conversation with her. Numb though she had been, she had realized that nobody in the village was speaking to her. At the borehole most women kept away from her. It's not that Winyo wanted to engage in conversation with anyone, but it still hurt to be shunned. And for what? She didn't completely know the rumours that were circulating in the village, but she knew she had to lie low for a while. Hence, Ader had temporarily taken over tending to the shop.

"You don't seem happy," Guma observed quietly as she kept on staring blankly at the paper that he extended to her. "What is the problem? Trouble at home?"

"It doesn't matter. You wouldn't be able to help." Nobody could help.

"Maybe, but we don't know that yet, because you haven't shared the problem. I may surprise you. And in the event that I can't help, the least I can do is listen," he said gently.

Winyo sighed wearily. She hated her state of mind. It had been two weeks and she had hoped the pain would have at least dulled by now, but no such luck. It still burned like a forge in her chest. She wanted an escape from her body; she felt dirty, stained. She bathed nearly five times a day now, but the filth seemed to cling to her like a paint on a wall. She couldn't wash it off, even the air she inhaled felt stained. She needed an escape, from herself, from her mind.

Guma was saying something that she missed completely. "What did you say?"

His entire face softened with concern. "How big is this problem?"

"I should get going, the borehole is still very far away from here and my mother will make a noise if I delay unnecessarily."

"Okay," he said slowly as he stepped out of her path.

Retrieving the jerrycan she had dropped on the ground, she walked around him with the intention of getting away but she had not prepared for the pang of loneliness that hit her the instant she had her back turned to him. It had been his kindness, Winyo realized. It had given her a temporary reprieve from her turmoil. He was the only one who had been remotely kind to her in the two weeks. Her friends, the twins, had been made by their parents to stay away from her. Acholla had gone to Kitgum town on an errand. She had been lonely.

Winyo paused and turned back, Guma was studying her hesitant retreat. If anyone knew what being shunned was like, it would be him. He probably hadn't heard the recent village rumours about her. She found herself wondering if he would not speak to her if he heard.

"Guma," she started slowly, and the next words died in her mouth. She didn't know how to ask him to stay with her, to keep her company and chase away the gnawing bleakness.

"Yes?" he prompted. "Please ask me to come with you."

Winyo couldn't help the smile that tugged at her lips at his playful plea. "Would you like to walk with me, if you are not doing anything awfully important?"

The grin he gave her was dazzling and Winyo once again found herself struck by the beauty of his face. "I am glad you asked. It would be my honour to escort you to your destination."

Winyo laughed. "I am just going to the borehole, not a dance."

"I am still honoured," he said with a grin as he fell in step beside her. "So, do you go to the borehole every day and tend to the shop as well?"

"Not currently but, yes, that is usually the structure of my day. I have to fetch water for the house. The shop is the easy part, I get to sit around for the whole day. Come to think of it, that's the only duty my brothers insist on doing," Winyo explained. "Sometimes I go to the field too, depending on the season."

"Wow you go to the fields as well." He sounded impressed as he said, "I could say you are by far the hardest working girl that I have ever met."

His praise was like a balm to her achy heart. "Thank you for saying that. Most people would disagree with you. Some would call me slow, lazy."

"Anyone who calls you that most definitely doesn't know you," he said easily.

"And you do?"

"I admit that I don't," he said then added earnestly, "It is very obvious that you work hard for your family. Anyone who can't see that is an idiot."

Winyo chuckled. "That idiot would be my mother."

"Oh–I …didn't mean …" he stuttered as he tried to back track but stopped as Winyo broke into pearls of laughter.

He then said, "By that I am taking that my mindless blunder is forgiven?"

"There is nothing to forgive. My mother thinks I am the worst daughter that could have ever been given to her."

"Why would she think that?" he asked incredulously, "You are amazing."

Winyo's gaze snapped to his, but his face was solemn. He was not mocking her, he truly thought she was amazing. Winyo couldn't help the flutter that skittered through her and once again he managed to so easily extract a smile from her bleeding heart.

"My mother has her reasons."

"Speaking of your mother, she has become the second owner of our house lately. Which brings me back to my original question, where have you been? I don't even see you at the shop anymore."

"I am not allowed to go there. For the time being, anyway," she said, basking in the knowledge that someone had actually noticed her absence. She had to admit, it had been a good idea asking Guma along. She was beginning to feel a lot better already.

"What did you do?" he asked.

"Things."

"Okay," he said. He wasn't eager to press her on the topic and for that she was grateful. "I hate that dress," he said after some time, taking her by surprise. She looked down at what she was wearing and once again couldn't help the laughter that burst out. It was a different dress from her usual. She was down to two dresses; she had burnt her old brown one, it had been the one she had worn when…Winyo quickened her steps. She didn't want to think about Uncle Saul.

Guma kept in step with her. "How about you come with your mother the next time she comes to our house?"

Going to the Odyek house, images of witch's potions and dark corners with white floating brooms flooded her mind. She shivered, rubbing her hands over the skin of her arms. How was it possible that even in her rattled state of mind she still had the space left for irrational fear?

She looked over at Guma; he seemed normal enough. He was nice, the only person who wanted to be civil to her. He was even giving her compliments.

"What do you go to do in the bushes?" she decided to ask, and she could tell her question had caught him off guard.

"Well, I go to draw and paint sometimes."

"Alone?"

He was amused. "Do I need someone?"

"Well, I mean- your brothers…"

He threw his head back and laughed. "Those guys wouldn't know how to hold a pencil even if they had a thousand lessons. I am afraid if

I ask them to come with me, they would take it as a punishment."

"Well, some people think you go to do other…things."

He turned to look at her profile; she trained her gaze on the ground. "I have heard the stories," he said eventually, "Quite an imagination people have, it is amazing."

Winyo frowned at the ground. What had she expected? That he would split open and confess that he and his entire family were indeed the witches doctors that everyone was terrified of? Now that would have been amazing.

"You believe them?" he asked

"Believe what?"

"Well, the 'things'?" he teased, as he made air quotes, but she could read the note of serious inquiry behind his jest. Taking in a long shaky breath, she let her eyes drift down to the main path that they had moved away from.

They were now on the small footpath. The borehole was only a few paces away. Winyo could hear the voices of the women down there and the metal sound of the borehole pump as someone worked on withdrawing water.

The cool smell of water-soaked clay filled the air. She had always liked that smell. In conversation, they had stopped unconsciously in a secluded area, only long waist high grass was beyond the path. It took her only a micro second to take all this in, and just as such, cold laced terror set in. She panicked. She was in an isolated place, again, with a male. It was all too familiar, all too wrong.

He must have noticed the terror that zipped through her, for, he immediately went on high alert, his gaze darting about. 'Winyo, what is it?'

"I–I should go–"

He took hold of her hand which only made it worse. Her pulse shot up to her throat and blood rushed up to her ears with a deafening roar.

"Let me go!"

"Okay, I will," he said but he didn't. "Just tell me, what is wrong? Are you okay?"

She started struggling against his hold, but he was strong- *oh no...no...no...* not again! She planted her feet on the ground in a bid to push away from him. He easily turned her round and was holding her with her back pressed against him, his arms locking her arms to her person. Cold memory sliced her like a knife in the gut, rage flooded her body like an ancient being.

Uncle Saul trapping her, Uncle Saul... Uncle Saul... She screamed so loud she was sure the next village heard her.

Then she was fighting at him in earnest.

"Winyo!!" The introduction of the new voice seemed to lift the haze in her mind. He approached from the direction of the main path. It was Okeny, her brother's friend.

"Winyo, what is going on here?" he demanded. Winyo glanced around her in panic. She was lying on the muddy ground, Guma had let her go at some point during the struggle. He now sported scratches on his face and his shirt was askew with buttons missing. Oh gosh! Had she done that to him? He had been trying to...hadn't he? Oh heavens, had she just assaulted the one person who was being nice to her?

Her mind was reeling like a freight train. Winyo staggered to her feet before finding her balance. She was gasping for breath.

"We were just talking...then she started ...fighting?" Guma answered, ending his explanation with a question directed at her. "Why did you attack me, little bird?"

"Odyek!!" Okeny bellowed. "Get your filthy paws off my woman!"

"What?" Guma asked in confusion his gaze swiveled from Winyo to Okeny and back again.

Okeny roughly yanked Winyo to himself. "She belongs to me, hear that? You have no place getting any of our women."

"Winyo, you have a boyfriend?" Guma asked as he rolled to his feet, his angry gaze bouncing between the two of them.

"So, you are the one," Okeny said in confirmation, "I should have known. The man that Winyo comes to see at the borehole? Ehh?"

What? Did he think? Winyo could read the same puzzled expression on Guma's face. She was still shaking, trying to recover from the panic attack that she had just had.

"I do not meet anyone at the borehole," Winyo answered quickly.

"And you... you." He turned at her, visibly shaking with fury, a finger pointing to her face. "Have you no shame at all?"

"What?"

"Leave her alone, I have never touched her," Guma spoke for her. "You have no right to speak to her that way."

Okeny wheeled at Guma, shoving him at the shoulder. "How dare you try to corrupt her?! What spell have you put her under?"

"I don't need a spell to get any woman." Guma shoved him back so hard Winyo had to step out of the way as Okeny clumsily gained back his footing.

Winyo stumbled again as she got pushed out of the way. Some sense made her notice that the voices of the people at the borehole had gone silent. No doubt curiosity was picking at them, and they wanted to hear every word of what was said. It would only be a matter of minutes before they ran up the path to witness what was going on. That would not be good. Not at all.

"Guys, please? Stop this!" Winyo hushed desperately as she wedged herself in between the two males. Guma easily moved her out of the way. Then they were at each other's throats again, throwing punches and fighting like wild animals as they rolled on the ground.

Further attempts at breaking up the fight only earned her a tumble in the grass and a bleeding nose. The two seemed to have forgotten all about her. Soon, people did come running from the borehole to find out the cause of the commotion.

It took three women to break the two men apart. By that time, nearly everyone who had gone to the borehole that day was present. They formed a circle around the three of them.

Blindly Winyo searched for an escape route, but the women that she bumped into held her in place- obviously taking her as the root cause of the fight- which was not entirely untrue.

"What is the matter with you, fighting over a girl?" a woman scolded, "What has become of our men?"

"Is that the girl you are fighting over?" The woman holding Guma jabbed a finger at Winyo's direction.

"They are not fighting over me," Winyo said quickly.

"Is that true?" The question was chorused at the guys who seemed like they wanted to have another go at each other, but the women holding them kept them firmly in place.

"That girl belongs to me," Okeny started. "And I found this pervert laying his filthy paws on her."

"That's not true!!" Winyo shouted.

"Shut up you!!" A large woman bustled into the centre of the circle; it was Aketo, her mother's friend, the village gossip. Winyo knew she was doomed the moment the woman's eyes lit up with recognition. The gods were truly cruel.

"You should be ashamed of yourself," Aketo started in a voice that dripped with censure.

"I didn't do anything!" Winyo persisted even as she came to the realisation that once again, her words held no weight.

"So, we are to believe that these boys just wanted to kill each other- for no reason?" Aketo said incredulously.

"Okeny misunderstood the situation," Winyo explained, and it sounded lame even to her ears. She could see the disbelief in everyone's face.

Then there was a bustle of voices as the crowd began talking at once. *"The girls of today..."* someone said. *"...they learn these bad manners from the town,"* another added. *"Oh, she studies in town, now does she...?"* *"...yes, the daughter of Gildo..."*

Aketo drew in a long, suffering breath and spoke again to Winyo. "Didn't your parents just recently beat you up black and blue for sleeping away from home with a married man?"

The din that arose from the crowd was deafening. Prompted by the crowd of sneering women, Aketo delved into the tale of how Winyo had shamed her parents by spending 'weeks' away from home, whoring herself out.

"This has to be taken to the clan elders," someone said. "Where is her mother...?"

Winyo's terror level hiked mountains high at the mention of her mother. Ader would surely kill her this time if she heard about this. *Okeny*, she thought darkly as she let the maddened crowd drag her home.

This time it was worse when she got dragged into the middle of her home compound. Ader had been so furious with her. She had let Okeny whip her - to teach her a lesson. Okeny for his part seemed delighted, even excited as he brought down the stick to whip her bottom.

By the time she was allowed to leave, she could barely sit straight and her entire body ached. She crawled into her bed and cried herself to sleep.

Sometime in the night she woke at the sound of scraping at her window. She successfully ignored it until she heard Guma's voice. "Winyo, are you okay? Talk to me, little bird."

She bolted out of the bed, too stunned to care about the sting on her abused body. She dashed to the small wooden window and flung it open.

"What the hell are you doing here?" she hissed at him, "Are you trying to get me killed?"

Under the bright moonlit night, his face was bathed in regret and worry. "I needed to make sure that you are okay. Can I come in?"

"You are trying to get me killed."

He ran a frustrated hand through his hair. "I don't mean to cause you anymore trouble, but I just need to make sure that you are well. I will draw more attention standing outside your window in the middle of the night than if I were inside."

Winyo was not sure that she was ready to let him inside her hut, but the thought of one of her parents discovering him at her window had her scrambling back to let him in.

"How did you know that this was my hut?"

"I was watching the homestead," Guma explained as he leapt into the room. He left the window slightly ajar so that the moonlight poured into the room. They stood staring at each other, separated by a golden beam of moonlight.

"Why?" she asked when he kept on staring at her, shame, concern and then anger tightening the lines on his face as he registered the extent of her bruises.

"I want to kill them for doing this to you!" Guma snarled as he reached out to trace the welt on her exposed neck. She was still in the dress she had worn, but the weak fabric was now shredded in several places; it was unsalvageable. She was now down to one dress to her name. She would now probably have to wear her school uniform if she ever did laundry on that one dress.

Stepping away from Guma's hand, she asked again, "Why were you watching my homestead?"

"Winyo," Guma cooed softly, the utter devastation in his voice made her feel like crying all over again. "I saw what they did."

"Everything?" she asked shakily. She hadn't wanted him to bear witness to her humiliation as well.

"Everything," he said gently, his eyes melting into hers. She attempted to drop her gaze but he wouldn't let her. "I tried to help you. You have to know that I tried to help. They just wouldn't let me get to you."

"You did?" Her voice wobbled as her heart clenched with emotion. He had tried to help her? He had not abandoned her. He knew nothing about her, but he had fought for her. Guma, whom she had gossiped shamelessly about alongside everyone in the village, was the only one to stand up for her.

"I am sorry," she whispered.

"What in the name of the gods are you sorry about?"

"For judging you and gossiping about you," she said, "You are obviously the only decent person that I know."

"Don't apologise to me, little bird," he said, "Not when I let this happen to you. Some of the men from the village held me back when I tried to get to you. I wanted to kill Okeny for hurting you, and your father for letting him do it. What kind of a father lets that happen to his child? He is supposed to protect you!"

The tears finally made their way down her cheeks. She did not deserve this coming from him. "My father has his reasons."

"Bullshit!" he snapped, "Okeny will pay for this, I will make sure of it."

Shaking her head, Winyo dragged herself to the mattress on the floor and sank down brokenly. "Leave it alone."

"I can't," said Guma as he came to sit beside her and together, they stared out of the window. "If I hadn't insisted on keeping you company today, you would have gone about your day as usual and none of this would have happened."

"You are not responsible for the bad things that happen to me."

Sighing, he fished inside his pocket and withdrew a small metal tin and after opening it, a strong minty smell wafted into the room.

"It is a cream medication that will help with the bruises and cuts," Guma explained as he scooped out some of the cream. "Let me rub this on for you. It is the least that I can do."

Too tired to object, Winyo said, "Just the ones on my arms and back, I can put the rest on in privacy."

Slowly and with aching gentleness, Guma started administering to her cuts and bruises. Winyo swallowed the lump that clogged the back of her throat, at his tender care.

"You don't even know me," she said. He stilled for a while as if processing her words before continuing on.

"I know you are reserved around strangers, your friends seek your company, so you are kind, you are loyal, and you are the most hard-working person I know," he recited. "I do know some things about you, little bird. I feel awful that I contributed to this happening to you." Finishing with her back, he slowly turned her to face him. "I am so very sorry, Winyo."

That apology floored her. His words touched the deepest part of her and this time she could not hold back the tears as she buried her face in her hands. He drew her to his lap and his arms locked around her in a manner that was so intimate it should have frightened her, but instead it made her feel protected, wanted by him, even loved, she dared dream as she sobbed into his shirt.

She wasn't sure how long they stayed like that, but when she finally did quiet down, a new awareness dawned on her. They both seemed to come to the same realisation at the exact same time. She was sitting on his lap with one leg near wrapped around him. Her thin dress and his jeans did not serve as much of a barrier because she could feel him, against her, growing thick and hard.

Winyo froze as she thought of words to make light of the situation, but it was hard to think clearly when he held her like this. She decided to just move away but wiggling to get free only resulted into their lower bodies coming more in contact.

His hold now felt like it had changed, as if he was no longer keeping her in place but holding her, embracing her. Her stomach dipped as she slowly lifted her gaze to his, he stared down at her, the lines against his mouth taut as the silence stretched on for long, delicious eternity. She knew that she should demand that he let her go but her mouth didn't want to form words.

Words still failed her when he lifted his fingers to trace the soft line on her chin with the pad of his thumb. This was possibly the sweetest torture that she would allow herself to feel. She needed this. She deserved this.

Guma hesitated. Winyo wondered if he was waiting to see what she would say, and when she still didn't object to his tender touch, his eyes shifted to a fierce burning brown. His hands slowly traced the skin on her cheek bone, then her neck. Her skin hummed with electricity as his eyes followed the path that his fingers took. His chin dipped as he lowered his face to hers, there was intent in the way his lashes lowered as he leaned in. He was going to kiss her, Winyo thought moments before his lips touched hers. Pleasure exploded in her gut as he plunged his tongue into her mouth. She sank into him as his fingers tangled with her hair, dominating her. There was a hunger in the intense way he devoured her mouth; her heart beat wildly in her ears as he crushed her to him, pulling her so tight to him that there was barely any space left. As if he, too, craved the intense heat as much as she did. His tongue tangled with hers as he chased away the darkness and replaced it with hot molten pleasure. It burned through her and pooled between her legs as she ground against him. He groaned in response as his fingers dug into her waist.

Too soon the kiss ended, and they were both panting. He held her gaze as he said raggedly, "I am sorry, I don't mean to take advantage of your vulnerable state, but I have been thinking about doing that for a while now. I should probably leave before I take this any further than you are willing to go."

Winyo nodded slowly as she fought to catch her breath, his words registering in her mind.

"Will you let me see you again, tomorrow?" His voice was rough in contrast to the soft touch that he trailed against her neck and the lingering kiss at her temple. A pulse of warm heat spread through her as he leaned his forehead to hers, their breath mingling.

"Say you want to see me again, little bird," he whispered hoarsely.

"I will see you again," Winyo replied, and she felt him smile.

"I must go now," he said.

"I know," Winyo replied but she did not move. She knew that the moment that he was gone, the spell would be broken and she would be back on her own, with her tortured soul and bartered body. This moment would be just that, a moment.

A moment where he was just a boy and she was just a girl, and he was not the son of the village witch and she was not the village branded whore.

So Winyo stayed longer on his lap because she knew that nothing would become of this attraction that she felt toward the Odyek son, no matter how intense or earth shattering it was.

6

It was four in the afternoon, but it was so gloomy that it was nearly dark from the heavy rain clouds that weighed overhead like preying phantoms, leaving the atmosphere dark and forbidding.

Of course, trivial things as a brewing storm were of no concern to her mother. She had inspected Winyo's bruises and after confirming that she was suitably healed, she had announced that they were going to the Odyek residence.

Winyo was surprised that they had reached their destination before the start of the rain although the wind blew so hard at the trees that they bent precariously on one side. The rain was the least of her concerns though. Guma was her main worry. She had successfully avoided him for the past two days. She was too much of a coward to bear his inevitable rejection. He must have by now come to the realization that what they shared had been a mistake and a heat of the moment kiss.

She refused to delude herself that Guma would want to be with her. She was not the kind of girl that guys like Guma wanted. She was plain and she didn't have a sparkling personality to make up for what she lacked in her looks. He had simply been feeling sorry for her that night and had taken things further than maybe he intended. She was sure he was regretting it now.

So, to avoid having to endure his apology, Winyo had resorted to sharing the room with her brothers, to avoid Guma if he came knocking at her window.

Today, she kept her eyes to the ground as they trekked down the dusty path to the grand house; she nearly lost her nerve. She had hoped by some miracle that they would not get there or that she would die on the way or something, but no such luck.

"You will go in and apologize to the family in a proper manner and pray to the heavens that you get forgiven for your despicable acts," Ader smartly dictated to her daughter in a low clipped tone.

Winyo balled her hands into a fist as she tried to shield her dread from her mother. Any additional suffering on her part would most definitely bring her mother satisfaction and despite everything, pleasing her mother was the last thing that she wanted.

Ader had dragged her all the way to come 'apologize' to Guma for causing him unnecessary embarrassment with her 'childish' games of deceit. She had been advised to claim a number of despicable things, so gruesome and emotionally destructive that Winyo couldn't help but wonder what mother would want her daughter to be portrayed in such a manner, then she remembered that this was Ader, and nothing came between Ader and her money. The Odyeks were a business opportunity and she was not messing with that.

The lights were on at the house, signifying the presence of the occupants. The knock on the huge wood door echoed inside her mind like a thousand empty rooms.

"You better get your act together," Ader hissed when sound of bolts on the other side of the door rattled before it creaked open.

Paul peeked out. "Ader, nice to see you, we weren't expecting you today," he spoke first, then his eyes drifted behind her. "Is that you, Winyo?"

"It is her," Ader confirmed, "I wish we were here under better circumstances."

Winyo watched as confusion took over his features, then alarm. "What is wrong?" he asked.

"I am sure you have already heard about the unfortunate events that happened at the borehole two days ago ..." Ader began.

"We have," he confirmed as he folded his arms across his chest.

"I am sure Guma was a perfect gentleman to her," Ader started, "but Winyo involved her boyfriend Okeny and...well, she is here to give an apology to your family."

"Okay..." Paul started to say before Ader interrupted him.

"Perhaps we should take this inside?" Taking Winyo's hand in hers, she blew past Paul and was into the living area in the space of a blink, as if she owned the place.

Winyo then got her first look at the inside of the Odyek house and her jaw dropped. Luxury dripped from the very corner of the house. The drapes were thick and expensive, the lounge chairs were covered in silky smooth cream upholstery. Large paintings hung on the walls, paintings probably done by Guma. A large round table made of black glass occupied the centre of the rooms, flowers had been placed at every corner of the room and miniature sculptures occupied the open spaces between the sofas. The living room was spacious and it was joined to a wide dining room with the same ease at which all the objects settled in the room. Winyo had never seen such luxury all in one place. It's no wonder that Ader wanted to get her claws hooked deep into these people.

A painting caught her eye. A mural of a forest, skillfully painted in shades of green and orange on the wall of the dining room with branches of the trees marrying with the flower vases around it. It was stunning.

"Call everyone in here right now. I need your mother here, your uncle too, if he is present and all your brothers," Ader dictated, temporarily the mistress of the residence.

Paul looked amused as he came to join them in the living room. "Yes, Ma'am," he quipped as he leaned towards the open corridor and bellowed, "Okwera! Guma! Earnest! Oyeng! Get your lazy backsides down here! Now! We have visitors."

"And your mother as well," Ader primly dictated.

"Someone, wake up Mom. She is needed too!"

Sure enough there were answers shouted back. Earnest hopped in, shrugging a sweater on his broad shoulders, followed by Guma. Surprise registered on their faces as they took note of the visitors who had interrupted their afternoon.

"Winyo?" Guma spoke first in a tone so shocked that had her wondering if he was disappointed or surprised. She could not tell; his features were guarded. She sighed in frustration; he probably was miffed that she was at his house. Maybe she should have spoken to him earlier on and got this awkwardness out of the way, but how was she to know that her mother would come up with this ridiculous idea, which would undoubtedly take this weird situation to a whole new level? He would surely not speak to her after today. Suddenly Winyo didn't know what to do with her hands. She nervously fidgeted with the hem on her sleeve as she looked everywhere but at him.

"What are you doing here?" he asked in a tone so gentle that she wanted to drown.

Ader took the liberty to respond in gushing streams of empathy that would put the Pope out of his job. "Guma, I am so deeply sorry and appalled at what you had to endure the other day all because of this…this…" Ader waved her hands at Winyo in dismissive gestures.

Winyo bit her lower lip, fixing her stare on the ground, once again letting the humiliation wash past her as she desperately tried to separate her emotions from the present. She wanted to get out of there– run away. She took in a deep breath to choke down the tears that stung the back of her eyes. *I am not going to cry*, she chanted to herself, *I will not cry*.

"What exactly is the problem?" The concern rang clear in Paul's question.

"Winyo will explain– as soon as your mother gets here," Ader confirmed as she dragged Winyo further into the living room and without invitation, perched herself on one of the chairs. Winyo was not too sure about sitting on the plush chairs in her dirty dress; she had not washed it in days. However, a glare from Ader had her scuttling to plonk on the edge of the nearest seat.

"Winyo?" Guma called for her attention. Winyo nodded but intently studied the ground. She just couldn't bear to make eye contact.

"Winyo," he repeated softly as he came to stand beside her. "What is this about?"

She didn't know how she could answer that without crumbling into a sobbing mess. The traitorous tears were so close to the surface that it was taking all her will power to hold them in.

"Winyo!!" her mother spat out through clenched teeth, "He is speaking to you."

Drawing in a deep calming breath, Winyo said, "It is about what happened at the borehole…"

Before she could elaborate more, they were interrupted by the entrance of Alice Odyek with Oyeng and Okwera, her youngest son providing for her support. The other boys sprang into action, Paul took her shoulder and guided her to a seat, Guma fluffed the cushions. They all fussed about their mother as they gently set her down. She was still battling the last effects of malaria. Alice for her part didn't look as weak as her sons seemed to make, in any case she looked more frustrated and kept on emphasising to her sons that she was not a 'baby.'

"What is this about?" Oyeng asked as soon as everything looked settled with their mother.

Ader sprung up like a daisy and was at Alice's side in a flush, gushing like a fountain over the woman's health. "My dear, dear friend, I would have been back here sooner if I had known how badly ill you were."

Alice scoffed, "I am not that ill, just a mild case of malaria, and I am much better already."

"Oh! you poor, poor darling, it cannot be easy, just remember that I am here for you if you need anything," Ader pledged, "You should not be going through this alone," Ader added as if Alice had a terminal illness.

Alice who clearly didn't like being treated like an invalid, sighed wearily and said, "I am not exactly alone. My overly protective sons are here with me, and besides I am much better already. Hope you don't take this the wrong way, but we were not expecting you today. You are still going to help us with the wedding arrangements, aren't you?"

Ader's next words were bordering on worship as she poured out her eternal devotion to Alice and her family. "You need not even question it, anything you need, just let me know."

"Thanks, Ader, I appreciate that," said Alice. She seemed to pause and glance out through the window. "Is it going to rain?"

"Yes, Mom, there is a storm just waiting to start," replied Earnest who was standing by the window.

"What a time to pay a visit, Ader," Alice commented. "Did something happen?"

"I should have come earlier, I know," Ader began in a very contrite tone, "This is one of the reasons that I have not been here to see you in the last few days. It has been weighing heavily on my soul." Ader paused for effect as she pressed her hand to her chest. Winyo was sure Ader would lose plenty of sleep at the thought of not getting any part of the money that the Odyek family would spend on the wedding.

"Goodness gracious, Ader," Alice said in alarm, "What is the problem?"

Having properly built up the tension in the room, Ader gestured to Winyo and Winyo thought she would surely throw up, when all eyes in the room were turned towards her.

Where to begin…where to begin? Where-to-begin?

In a rush of words, Winyo stuttered through the story of how she was going to the borehole and persuaded Guma to walk with her- yes 'persuade' was the word Ader had insisted that she use. Then Winyo explained how she had found a secluded area and started to seduce Guma before her boyfriend Okeny found them out. By the end of the fiction tale, Guma's face was a mask of fury. As she had spoken, his face had gone from surprise to shock, to disbelief then anger so potent that he looked like he was vibrating with it.

"What the hell, Winyo?" he demanded, his words like ice chips.

Winyo couldn't look at him, she instead glanced at her mother who levelled her with a speaking glare. Oh yes…Winyo remembered she had forgotten the apology part of her instructions. Winyo then rattled out the apology that her mother had made her rehearse on their way here. It contained of mostly how sorry she was that she had caused trouble between their two families and how she would do everything in her power to make sure that they put this juvenile issue behind them. Silence filled the room as her story came to an end.

Earnest whistled into the tense silence that followed. "Guma, you didn't think to check if she was single–or not?" he teased.

Winyo could feel Guma's searching gaze on her, and she eventually turned to face him and immediately regretted it. He looked disappointed.

"I am very sorry for what happened," Winyo repeated.

His voice broke when he asked, "Are you sorry for– all of it?"

She knew he meant the kiss in her room. He wanted her to apologise for that too? But *he* had come into her room. Surely, he didn't regret it that badly that he wanted *her* to issue an apology. Or had she been the one who initiated the intimacy in her muddled state of mind to? Winyo couldn't remember anymore. Maybe she did owe him an apology for that too. She had known that he would, to some extent, try to distance himself from her, but this, this was too much. The pain that spiraled through her was mind numbing. Winyo carefully tucked the broken pieces of her heart as she fully faced Guma.

"I am truly sorry for my behaviour. I will not be that forward with you ever again," she emphasized the last bit to get her meaning to him.

"For crying out loud, Winyo," Paul sighed, "this whole situation sounds more like Guma's fault than anything. Besides, it must have been embarrassing enough for both of you. I am sure no one blames you."

"There is nothing to blame," Guma growled angrily. "No one in my family blames you for anything. I most definitely don't blame you for anything."

"We should put all this behind us," Alice said quietly. "What ever happened was unfortunate, but my boys are tough. I am sure Guma can handle something as minor as village women gossip, right?"

Guma nodded stiffly, his eyes on Winyo.

"You are such a wonderful person Ader, but you take a lot of things too seriously," said Alice, "Children will do all sorts of stuff."

"Well, you don't need to worry about such a thing ever happening again," Ader assured her happily. "Now that all this is sorted, my daughter and I will be heading back home."

Ader had just risen to her feet when the steady flow of rain thundered on the iron sheet roofing. Winyo groaned and slumped back in her seat. She had hoped to be out of there as soon as she was done with the sordid story. No such luck.

"Thought I would find you here." Earnest's voice startled Winyo from her brooding.

She was huddled on the floor in the corner of the large kitchen. She had left everyone in the living area in search for the bathroom, and after she had not felt the need to go back into that room and face Guma's silent anger. She, for the life of her, couldn't fathom why he would be so furious with her. She had apologised, hadn't she? Isn't that what he had wanted? Her mind could not process complex thoughts.

Winyo had wandered into the kitchen and just crumpled on the floor at a shadowy corner. The magnitude of the kitchen only made her feel more exposed.

"Why are you looking for me?" she asked glumly.

He was holding a mug of tea that he waved under her nose. "Drink. It will make you feel better."

Sighing in resignation, Winyo took the cup and took a hesitant sip. Seemingly pleased, Earnest flopped on the floor beside her and said, "What happened today was completely unnecessary. Guma had already told us the story."

"Did he now?" Winyo wondered out loud. Had he told them everything? Gosh, had he told them of the kissing in her room as well? Winyo buried her face in her hands and groaned audibly.

"I didn't mean to get you uncomfortable," Earnest said, noticing her reaction.

"What did your brother tell you?"

"He certainly didn't go into as much detail as you did," Earnest said quickly as he noted her growing distress. "Winyo, I am disastrously trying to say that we do not blame you for anything that happened. You did not deserve to be disciplined by your boyfriend in front of a crowd. You should have told Guma that you had a boyfriend though. I am sure he must be feeling terrible for putting you in that situation."

"I don't have a boyfriend," Winyo sighed wearily as she leaned against the wall. "Okeny likes to think and act like he is my boyfriend."

Earnest studied at her profile for so long that Winyo said, "What do you want to say to me?"

"I was wondering why you don't have a boyfriend," he said, "You are quite attractive."

Winyo rolled her eyes.

"You don't believe me," he chuckled, "Why don't you believe me? Hasn't Guma ever told you that before?"

"What does he have to do with anything?"

"I think he finds you interesting," Earnest said. "Besides, he is an artist, he likes drawing pretty things, I figured that was why he kept seeking you out. I think he wants to draw you."

"Draw me?" Winyo couldn't hide the disappointment in her voice. "Is that all he wants?"

Earnest looked amused and the grin he gave was truly wolfish as he said, "I wouldn't speak for him but if he were given more encouragement, he could want to do much, much-"

"You should shut your trout," Guma's irritated voice startled both of them. Earnest laughed at the murderous expression on his brother's face as he crowded the kitchen door.

"Hey now, don't you know how to knock before you enter a room," Earnest protested in mock offence.

"It is a bloody kitchen," Guma snarled.

"Somebody is in a mood. Did you know that Okeny isn't Winyo's boyfriend?" Earnest continued breezily.

"It doesn't matter," Guma said through clenched teeth.

"Huh," said Earnest, "I can tell you it was good news to my ears.

Means she is single and since I am single …let's say I have a lot that I would like to share with her."

"I want to talk to Winyo. Alone," he added in a growl as Earnest looked to make himself comfortable.

"Are you sure? Because her mother is in the next room and considering–"

"Out!" Guma growled.

"Okay, I get it. See you Winyo." Earnest was on his feet with the biggest grin on his face. At the door he called back, "Winyo, in case you need me, just yell out, I will be right–"

"Out!" Guma thundered. Earnest's amusement lingered as he laughed himself out of the room.

Left alone with him, Winyo bristled. He slowly walked into the room and took up Earnest's vacated spot on the floor.

After a long silence he asked, "How are you, really?"

She felt heartbroken and the shards pricked at her soul. She wondered how long it would take before the last piece of her sanity burnt away with the constant pain of it all. Perhaps this was how lunatics came to be. They had one village mad man and he always walked naked and often seemed in deep conversation with himself. Would that be her fate too?

"I will be ok," she said instead.

"I think I hate your mother," Guma said.

Winyo nodded. "I can't say I love her very much at this very moment. However, I know why she is here today. I understand that she wants to work on the upcoming wedding and doesn't want to jeopardize the relationship with your family."

"Then you are a better person than I am," Guma said, "For what she has done to you alone, I want to insist that she gets barred from the wedding. But that would only hurt you. Your family needs the business."

"Thank you," Winyo said but it must have been the wrong thing because it only seemed to annoy him further.

"How are you so accepting of this whole situation?" he snapped.

"As opposed to what?" Winyo demanded.

"I don't know, speaking up? Not do everything your crazy mother wants. Hell! Defend yourself," he seethed. "You were beaten up so badly for some crap you didn't do, then you show up here and apologise to *me* of all people. Come on Winyo, you can't be that timid."

Winyo looked away, humiliation burning her face at the realization that he, once again, had found her lacking. She had always been timid; she didn't know how to change that. Ader was an indomitable force that she couldn't push against. She couldn't do any of those things he said. Ader would surely become more inventive with her punishments if she dared go against her.

"My mother is usually a nice person; she just doesn't like it if people go against her and she most certainly does not like being gossiped about in the village if she isn't controlling the story."

"And you are all too happy to be her punching bag."

She swallowed hard and turned away. There was a lot of truth in everything he was saying, but she wasn't exactly happy about it. A lecture from him was the last thing she needed right now. She was already beating herself into a pulp; she didn't need his help crushing her spirits any further. Embarrassingly enough, she felt the pain prick at the back of her throat and the definite watering effect at the back of her eyes that signified the onset of tears.

"Please stop," she said softly but her voice cracked as she tried to hold back the tears. Immediately she was in his arms. He drew her to his lap and wrapped his arms around her, burying her face against his chest. Her shoulders shook as the sobs wracked her body. Apparently, she was unable to hold back her emotions around him. Even when she was whipped black and blue, she had always kept the tears at bay. But faced with his angry defence of her, she easily crumpled like a paper in water.

"I am sorry, hush now," he cooed as he ran his hands through her hair. "I don't mean to make you cry. It hurts me to see you treated this way."

"It is fine," she sniffed.

"No, it is not," he refused. "How can I help? Tell me how I can help you, and I will do it."

The sincerity in his voice tugged at her broken heart strings and darn near unraveled her again.

"Just hold me, Guma," she said. And he did just that. He held her long after her tears had dried up and long after the rain had ceased.

"I got something for you," he said into her hair. "Wait here."

Guma left the room and moments later came back with a small paper parcel. Winyo opened it to reveal three beautiful pastel-coloured dresses.

"I figured that you deserved something nice," Guma said to her bent head. "Do you like them?"

Her heart constricted almost painfully with emotion. She nearly burst out into tears again. Clearing up her throat, she pushed back the lump that clogged the back of her throat. How do you thank someone who saw you more clearly than even your parents did? How do you thank someone who responded to your needs with such abundant kindness and expected nothing in return?

"I like them," she said gratefully. "Thank you, Guma."

"Don't worry, I made sure your mother knows that they are gifts from my mother," Guma added. "It's not completely untrue because she helped me pick the dresses."

Placing his finger on her chin he tipped up her face. "Where is my smile?" he asked tenderly.

Winyo couldn't resist the wonky smile that tugged at the corner of her lips.

"That's much better. Promise me that you will try to smile as often as you can."

"I will keep smiling."

"Good girl," he whispered as he bent down to lean his forehead against hers. She inhaled his warm scent as she quickly discovered that she loved being the sole focus of his attention. Her pulse quickened as he languidly rubbed his nose against hers like a cat, sending sparks of electricity through her skin and coiling deep into her core. She didn't attempt to ignore the carnal hunger that circulated through her system as he tilted her head back further and brushed a light kiss on her lips.

She tried not to be disappointed as he drew back but she knew she hadn't succeeded in hiding her thoughts when he said, "Winyo, believe me, I would like nothing more than to devour your luscious lips and hold you in my arms all day, but I don't want to get you in more trouble than you are already in. Your mother could walk in here any moment."

Nodding in agreement, Winyo stepped away from him and asked the question that had been plaguing her mind. "Do you like me?" No sooner had the words escaped her lips did she regret them. She sounded clingy- no, worse, desperate, but darn it! She couldn't figure out the reasons for his attentions, welcomed as they were.

"I am not the kind of girl that a guy like you would go for," she quickly added.

"And what kind of girl would a guy like me go for?" he parroted in amusement.

"You know- pretty, worldly, wealthy and from a good family. I am none of those things. I don't even have enough clothes for my back. I wouldn't choose me if I were a guy."

"Stop that," he growled protectively as he invaded her personal space again and took her face in his hands. "I see a humble, kind, gentle, tough girl who puts everyone before herself and she is as beautiful as the sunrise on the hills of Agoro. You are not just beautiful Winyo, you radiate light. You dazzle me, I have not been able to stop thinking about you ever since I first met you."

Her already putty heart melted even further. She desperately hoped he meant those words otherwise she was skipping around in real heartbreak territory.

"So, you like me," she said with a smile in her voice.

"Yes, little bird, I like you. A lot," he chuckled. He leaned forward and feathered another kiss on her lips that had her aching for more.

"I must take you back to your mother, before she comes looking for you."

Winyo groaned.

Winyo had spent the rest of the evening and the next day in a blissful bubble. Guma had stopped at the shop to have a chat. She had been thoroughly tempted to close the shop for the day when he had dragged her to the back room, hauling her against his body. He had proceeded to kiss her so possessively and thoroughly that she had forgotten herself. A knock at the shop door had alerted her to a customer.

Winyo had quickly attended to the little girl who had come to buy a bag of beans and sent her on her way.

"We need to be more careful," she said to Guma as he came up behind her and nuzzled her neck.

"Ok. I will see you tomorrow when you come to our place with your mother," he said. Winyo nodded and shooed him away. She didn't want him to leave, but she was not too keen on stirring up more gossip in the village.

She was still on cloud nine later that evening when it happened to her again. Perhaps this time it hurt more because it brutally yanked her from her state of loving bliss and dragged her back into the pit of darkness that Guma had successfully coaxed her out of, just the day before.

She was on her way home from the shop when she ran into Ronald and Okot. They were among the few students who she studied with in Kitgum town. She had stopped to talk to them- mistake number one.

Then she had allowed them to keep her talking till it was almost too dark to see a thing- mistake number two.

Then Okot had his hands on her arm. "Give us a taste of what you gave to the married man," he had said into her ear. "It has been driving me crazy ever since I heard about it. I heard that you know all sorts of positions."

"I heard that you are a wild one," Ronald smirked. "Are you a screamer like they said?" It was the sound of the unmistakable arousal in his voice and the invasion of her space that finally made the sirens break out in her mind. Before she could do anything, Ronald had taken possession of her other arm and plastered himself to her side. Their intentions, unmistakable.

"Let's make this fast and easy. There is no need to make this unnecessarily difficult," he had whispered into her ears. "You know you want this."

Winyo cursed at her luck and the depth of her stupidity. They had probably been standing at the side of the road, waiting for her to leave the shop.

She was no match for them, she had put up a brave struggle but, in the end, it was of no use. They had ripped at her new dress and dragged her into the bushes and taken her body roughly on the ground. She hadn't bothered to scream; this had seemed to please them for they had praised her endlessly about how much she liked it and what a good girl she was. But in truth she hadn't wanted any more witnesses to her shame. She would rather bear this alone. She did not want to call out to someone who would twist the story. Given her current history, nobody would believe that this was not consensual and her mother, oh her mother would surely disown her.

So, she had kept her mouth shut, and when they were done, they had thrown her tattered clothes at her and told her to cover up her whore body.

Winyo had bottled up her humiliation and slowly dragged herself home. She had changed into another dress and proceeded to making the family's evening meal. It was only after she was in the safety of her room that she had let the hot burning tears scorch her face. She cried until the sun dawned on another day.

She did not want to see the faces of Ronald and Okot in broad day light. She didn't think she would be able to handle it. The hurt and anger simmered way too close to the surface. She wanted them dead. She craved it like a drug. It was all she could think of. She indulged in fantasies of the different ways in which a human could be painfully killed and the victims always had Ronald and Okot's faces. She wanted them to suffer as they died, and she wanted her face to be the last thing they saw.

She had seen them once since that fateful evening. She had gone to deliver a message to Ader at the village market. Ronald and Okot were sitting with a group of men, Ronald had waved at Winyo, a leering grin on his face, and the entire group had burst out laughing. Winyo had seethed in anger. She knew what the laughter was about. The bastards had shared what they had done to her, and she was almost certain that there would be a lot of their friends waiting for an opportunity to try their luck with the new village whore.

She had been careful since then and stayed away from Ronald and

Okot. She avoided walking alone at all times. It sickened her beyond measure; it was she who had been violated and she was the one forced to hide like the criminal. At night she racked her mind on what she needed to do about the situation.

She had completely avoided going to the Odyek residence and made sure her brothers were always with her at the shop. She could not bring herself to face Guma. He might have wanted her before but she highly doubted that he would want her now, considering what she had allowed to happen to her.

She could not bring herself to hide it from him if he insisted on being with her, but that knowledge that she hadn't even bothered to cry out for help, and she had just laid down and taken it, burned at her. He would no doubt think that she had wanted it too. And for the life of her, she did not want to see his adoration of her wither and die from his eyes. That would surely kill her.

So, she avoided him. When he came to the shop, she let her brother attend to him. He had tried to talk to her, but she mumbled a few words before disappearing to the back room of the shop.

One afternoon she was at home, making the lunch time meal, her baby brother beside her, howling at the world like a deserted wolf, Acholla had come to visit. As usual she was piping with stories of how she had spent her days in Kitgum town.

Winyo contemplated how she could convey her problems to her friend. But after hours of listening to the vivacious and animated tales that Acholla was rattling about, she gave up hope. Acholla wouldn't help her. Acholla would be alarmed and insist on telling her mother who would tell someone, and the entire village would be up in her business again.

"Have you fed that child?" Acholla had asked as the baby howled even louder.

"I have fed it with anything and everything that a baby should eat,"

Winyo said as she heaved a long suffering sigh. Winyo was just about to tell Acholla about Guma when her friend suddenly went quiet. Winyo turned to look over her shoulder and there he was.

Uncle Saul.

He was wheeling his motorcycle into the compound, a gleeful smile curving up his lips as he took notice of her.

Stone cold fear crawled up her back and gripped her neck in a death vice. The memory of being tied up hopelessly as this man loomed over her, slammed into her mind. She trembled so hard that her feet could not hold her weight. She sank onto the ground.

The sauce pans dropped from Winyo's hands. "Oh my lord!" The words slipped out of her lips like the breath of a dying animal as her heart plummeted to her feet.

"Winyo, my beautiful bird!" he hailed gleefully.

7

"Bend," he had said as Winyo stood trembling before him.

Uncle Saul had followed her on her way to the borehole and dragged her into a private area in the bush.

Winyo shook her head in refusal; she knew what he wanted to do to her. He already had removed his belt and was rubbing his huge belly in anticipation of the pleasure that he intended to receive.

"Come on Winyo," he implored gruffly, "You know you have been longing for this as much as I have, considering how wonderful our last session had been."

Her stomach heaved with revulsion. She didn't want to just lie down and take it this time, not again. She could hear the voices of the women on the road. The bush shielded them from view, but she could tell they were many in number. Perhaps if she screamed really loud, she could get help.

"Don't even think about it," her uncle said, reading her turn of thoughts.

"I will scream," she threatened.

"I will only say I found you here with a lover and he ran off as soon as I arrived," he divulged. "Let's just save both of us that kind of embarrassment."

All the embarrassment would be on her. Winyo gritted her teeth in suppressed anger. Was there no solution to her dilemma? Was this her life now? Was this the cross that she was to bear? The path that she was to walk her entire life? She thought as despair and utter hopelessness sank into the pit of her stomach like a weighted stone.

No one would believe the story of her uncle trying to rape her. Even she could tell that Uncle Saul's version of the situation was more easily believable.

"Now, now Winyo, don't worry about it," he said with a conquering grin of someone who knew that he was about to get what he wanted. "I can guarantee that I will make you enjoy it. You remember how good I was to you the last time, don't you?"

"No," she said bravely but her knees were shaking so bad they knocked at each other. Accursed tears filled her eyes now and poured endlessly down her face. Then, degradingly, she started begging, "Please don't- Uncle, don't. If you have any love for my mother, you wouldn't do this."

He was moving to her, taking her by the hand. He yanked her to him. She was so crippled with fear she could barely keep herself upright. "Hush now my darling, you don't understand," he cooed, "I have love for your mother, but so much more for you, Winyo. Let me show you how much."

He tried to undo the button on her dress, but the sound of women's voices reached them again, much closer this time. Uncle Saul pushed her away from him. Winyo almost screamed in relief as Aketo and a group of her friends walked into their clearing. Winyo had no idea why the women were trekking off the main path but she was so grateful that they had. Aketo's face lit up at the sight of Uncle Saul, and Winyo took that opportunity to slip away while they were in conversation and ran.

She ran so furiously, not caring where she was going, but knowing that she had to get away. When she eventually slowed and then stopped, she was panting and still trembling so much that she crashed to the ground in a heap.

Winyo didn't know at what point it happened, but her grappling hands had found a thorn on the ground. Then she was lashing at the skin of her hands and arms. The pain that seared through her was like a breath of life and brought much needed relief from the soul tormenting pain that wrapped around her like a snake. The oozing blood dulled the pain but only for a second. She had to cut some more. So, she did. Over and over again. Then she was slashing deeper and deeper into the veins.

That was when Guma had found her.

"Winyo?!" he bellowed in horror. She registered the alarm and panic in his voice as he sprinted towards her. He yanked the thorn away from her and in a swift motion, was tying something around her arm. It took her a moment to realize that it was his shirt, as he was now only down to a vest.

"What in the hell's damned earth are you doing?!" he shouted, panic lacing his tone. "Do you want to kill yourself?"

"What brings you here?"

"What brings me here?!" he snarled incredulously. "I thought I saw a footpath and decided to use it. What in the hell are you doing here?"

When Winyo didn't speak, he attempted to gentle his tone, but it was still jagged with anxiety as he said, "Talk to me, little bird."

That endearment did it. She desperately clung to him. "I want to breathe. I ...can't breathe..."

He stared at her tear washed face, his brown eyes bouncing between hers as varied emotions raced across his features, alarm, concern, worry... Then he had folded her in his arms, and once again she had sobbed like a trout. He seemed to find her in such a mess so often it was not even funny.

It was evening when he walked her back home, carrying her empty water jerrycan. She hadn't even realized that she still had it. He did not ask any more questions about her distress.

Thankfully, her mother was nowhere in sight when they arrived at Winyo's home. It was only Atang making the fire for the evening meal as she rocked Winyo's baby brother.

"Perhaps you should talk to someone. My mother could help," Guma suggested as he handed her the jerrycan.

"There is no need," Winyo answered quickly.

He captured her chin with his fingers. She struggled to avert her eyes, but she caught the concern on his face and somewhere in that insanity in her mind, she felt him reach for her and find her.

"Winyo, you are obviously upset, you need to talk to someone," he spoke calmly. "If you won't speak to me, then talk to your mother."

"She won't listen."

"Okay, then bloody talk to me," he demanded impatiently.

"Winyo!" Atang called, "How long does it take you to get to the borehole and back? You surely took your time. Come over here, I need your help."

Guma shuffled restlessly on his feet. "Can I see you tomorrow? Let me see you tomorrow."

"No."

"The day after that then?"

"No, I don–"

"Darn it, Winyo!" he snapped in exasperation, "I need to make sure that you are well. Whatever it is that you are going through, you seem to be suffering it alone. What I saw today scared the life out of me, and I shudder to think of what would have happened if I hadn't found you. I will show up looking for you anyway, but it will be easier if you will let me speak with you."

"Why?"

"Why?" He stared at her as if she had lost her mind altogether. "I thought that would be bloody obvious: I am worried about you. I found you in the process of committing suicide. Am I supposed to forget about it and act like it was another day at the zoo?"

"I was not committing suicide."

"Okay, care to explain?"

"No."

"Tomorrow it is," he said. He waited till she nodded her consent before he turned and stalked away, clearly reluctant to leave because he kept glancing back as if he intended to come back.

Winyo watched his hesitant departure with mixed emotions. He had no idea how grateful she was for his care, though there was no way in a thousand years that she was going to tell him what she had been dealing with.

Guma had once demanded of her not to be timid. It was then that she decided that she had to put an end to this vulnerable person that she had become. She was going to be strong. She was going to defend herself.

"You look terrible," Guma informed her dryly the next day as he took stock of her puffy face and glum expression. "How are you feeling?"

She was at the shop alone. Her mother had gone to the garden, but not before leaving explicit instructions for Winyo not to embarrass herself and the family. Winyo couldn't wait for the holiday to end so that she would at least go back to her boarding school in Kitgum town. There she would at least get a break. Never had she wished so much to go back to school. Winyo spared Guma a brief glance before burying her head back in the record books.

"You are not making any more bicycle rides around the village?" Guma asked as he leaned against the counter.

She kept studying the books. "No."

"Is the reason for that the same as the reason for last night's incident?"

"In a way."

"Is it family trouble?" he persisted.

When she didn't reply he tried another approach, "Do you always cut yourself when you are upset?"

"No, I don't."

Winyo shook her head. She was making this conversation unnecessarily hard, and she knew that. The arrival of the twins halted his interrogation.

It had been a long time since she had seen their cute identical faces and Winyo was glad that they obviously had been cleared to speak with her.

"We hear the two of you have something going on," Acen sang.

What? Winyo quickly glanced at Guma; he looked startled, then amused.

"Yep, we hear, you are like this," Apio illustrated by twining her finger with her sister's. Guma laughed then.

"Now where did you hear that?" he asked.

"Come on, everyone is talking," Acen said, "So...?"

"So, nothing," Winyo said, "Why would anyone say we are like...that?"

"The news that Guma and Okeny were fighting over you is everywhere. Since you clearly don't like Okeny...so you and Guma sitting on a tree..." Apio sang.

"We have nothing going on...yet," Guma added and the twins squealed in delight. Winyo didn't understand why he was encouraging gossip about himself.

"Keeping it a secret..." That was Acen.

"I thought the whole point of a secret was that no one knew of it. How can it be a secret if everyone knows?" Apio asked, "Winyo, we are your friends, give us all the details."

Winyo said, "Speaking of friendship, I haven't seen the two of you in such a long time. Where have you been?"

"We have been here and there, listening to stories about you. Anyways, Guma, how is the wedding arrangement coming up?" Apio prattled on.

"We hear it is going to be the event of the year. Everyone is looking forward to it," Acen added.

"It's coming up okay. I didn't know people were looking forward to the wedding," Guma said. "What are they saying?"

Trust the twins to have gossip. In unison, they leaned over to Guma and were almost talking as one. "They say there is going to be food lined up to the footpath…"

"…no, that you are going to have a cake the size of a cow, imported all the way from Kampala, you know, like the cake that the King of Buganda had for his wedding…how far true is that?"

"…oh, shut up, they say that you are bringing a whole herd of cows for the dowry, that's true right?"

Winyo shook her head. "Even I know that is not true."

"Winyo's mother is helping a lot with the arrangements. We are buying cereals and flour from them," Guma answered.

"You are?" they chorused.

"Winyo, that means you won't have to get on your bicycle for a very long time," Apio said.

After a bit more happy chattering, the twins skipped off to the market. Both Guma and Winyo took a deep sigh as they returned to their conversation.

"Let's not talk about it," Winyo said quickly as Guma turned to her. He hesitated as if searching for the correct words to say. She knew he meant well. He must have assumed a lot of scenarios and possible reasons in his head by now, most of which would be close to the truth.

"Where are your brothers?" he asked instead, "Do they know of what happened to you?"

"Nothing happened," she insisted, "And I don't want to talk about it." She did want to tell him everything but telling him didn't solve anything. Her confession would only serve to drive him away from her.

"Somebody hurt you," he said. His face seemed to grow cloudy and still as he added, "Was it Okeny? Did he...did he touch you?"

She knew what he meant, the words he could not say. It was in the tension in his face and the rigid set of his shoulders. He was so close to the truth. He had just got the person wrong.

"It is not Okeny," she admitted quietly.

"It was someone then," he said through gritted teeth. "Who?"

"Leave it alone, Guma," she snapped. "It's not what you are thinking and I don't want to talk about it." She was not going to tell him how she let those nasty village boys use her body. Winyo shook her head to clear the dark images. She was so ashamed that it was Guma who found her in that state yesterday. Weak and broken. He seemed to only see her at her lowest points. Yet he was still here...

"I was not trying to kill myself," she said to him. "You don't have to worry about that. I just don't want to talk about it with you."

He slowly nodded with a frown on his face, probably sensing that he was getting nowhere at that moment. "The worst thing about a depression is that you begin to feel like you need to be pissed for a while, then a while becomes a little longer and believe me it is not cool."

Winyo spared him a glance. "You speak like you can relate."

He shrugged. "We all have our moments, Winyo. Everyone's life sucks at some point. Some more than others, but we each have a way to deal with it. How do you deal with your bad days, besides cutting yourself?"

Winyo shrugged. "I don't know, I suppose I just cry or suck it up."

He nodded in thought. "When I am upset, I draw– a lot, that is because I love drawing. What do you love?"

She shook her head. "I don't know."

"Ok," he drawled. "Maybe we can do what I like and see if it makes you feel better."

"I don't know how to draw."

"I could teach you how to draw- if you want," he added quickly.

Winyo cocked her head, as she studied his eager expression. Thick, warm emotion wrapped itself around her chest and spread throughout her body like warm honey. By the gods, he was beautiful! Not just his face, it was his soul was well. The deepest part of him that kept on reaching out to her time and time again, no matter the depth of her despair.

"Why are you being nice?" she asked.

He sighed wearily as he ran his hands through his hair. "Winyo..." he said her name imploringly. "No one should ever cry alone."

He leaned over the counter then and tilted her face to his, rubbing his thumb along her jaw as he said, "I won't lie to you, it scared the life out of me. I would give anything to take away the feeling that drove you to harm yourself like that. Promise me that no matter how bad it gets, you won't do that again. Promise me this."

Winyo nodded slowly, she could not speak. Emotion threatening to overwhelm her. She did not want to cry again, because she knew that he would take her in his arms again and soothe the pain away like he always did. She, however, also knew that he abhorred weakness. He wanted her to be strong. He did not like her timidity, and her tendency of always being in tears around him would surely grow old fast.

She was going to be strong from now on.

"Will you draw with me?" he asked gently, a smile tugging at the corner of his lips.

She nodded again. "I am afraid I can't even draw a circle."

He chuckled. "I have heard that a piece of paper and pencil can be quite the scary duo."

Winyo laughed despite herself.

"I draw really badly," she warned as he placed a pencil in her hand and tore up a clean sheet for her.

"Don't even worry about it, you will never get to draw as well as I can. Nobody can," he said with a teasing grin.

Again, Winyo couldn't help the laugh that bubbled up through her.

"Your humility is astounding," she replied.

"Thank you," he replied with a slight bow. "Lets start with something simple."

"What! right now?" she asked in alarm.

Grinning like a cat, he reached into his backpack and drew out a book and pencil.

"Let's start with something simple. How about...a cup." He placed her measuring cup on the counter. "Surely you must have drawn a cup at kindergarten," he teased.

Winyo rolled her eyes and bent over the paper. She knew she was terrible at this, but it seemed like something he would not let go, so she obliged with him. Minutes later, she presented the drawing to him.

"Goodness above, how old are you? Three?!" he exclaimed, "This is terrible! Horrible!"

"What? That was my best!" she protested.

"Oh Winyo, I have been told that I am an excellent educator, but in your case, I must say– I am no magician."

"Oh! shut it."

When he continued laughing at her, she grabbed a handful of the flour and sprayed it at him till he begged for her to stop and when she did, he promptly ducked under the counter took a handful of flour and showered her with it.

A bag of rice got knocked to the floor and their feet slipped on the grainy ground. They both collapsed on the floor laughing.

They spent the afternoon having more drawing lessons. Acholla joined them sometime during the afternoon and she too, was given a pencil. Her friend proved to be a better artist than she was and in no time, she had joined Guma in the jokes about her lack of artistic talent.

For the first time in a long while, she slept well through the night. She did not have to see Uncle Saul that night; he had gone to visit one of his friends and he came back long after everyone had gone to bed. She was grateful.

Guma met her on the way to the garden the next day. He helped her with the weeding of the finger millet. After cutting himself a few too many times with the weeding knife, he gave up and left her to it.

She had laughed the entire time. She had never thought it possible that anyone could hurt themselves with the curved weeding knives. They were sharp alright, but the hook like bend of the knives protected anyone from harm unless they performed it intentionally.

He had made some remarks about slave work and how machines had been invented to do such kind of work, and then he was gone.

Having him around complaining about manual labour had been the best part of her day. She had kept working in the field and late afternoon had found her heading back home but so had her Uncle Saul. He had found her.

Winyo's family field was unfortunately far away from any kind of homestead or main road. They had created a tiny footpath to the field but unfortunately, it was still several miles away from the main path. Vast bushy land surrounded them as far as the eye could see, and for once she clearly understood why her mother insisted that either she or her brothers came to the field with her. Today had been no exception but her brother Apach had chosen to go somewhere else with his friends despite her protests and threats of telling her mother. So unfortunate for her, she had had to carry two hoes and two weeding knives with the hope that her brother would change his mind and join her, but he hadn't.

Uncle Saul had known where she would be and had known that she would most likely be alone. He blocked her path like an omen of death. Cold dread sliced through her chest as her heart started racing. Her first instinct had been to run. Run away, but her feet were rooted to the ground.

"Winyo, I knew I would get you alone sometime," he drawled slowly as his eyes scanned the bushes around them as if to make certain that they were alone. Unfortunately, Winyo knew that they were totally alone. Guma had left several hours ago, and she knew she would only see him the next day, because that was what he had promised when he left.

"If I didn't know better," he began, "I would say that you were avoiding me."

Blood roared so loudly in her ears that she could barely think.

"I saw you with the Odyek boy in the morning, you should stay away from the likes of him," he continued, then his face hardened as a thought crossed his mind. "Are you letting him touch you?"

When she didn't answer, he strode towards her and yanked her onto his sweaty chest as his left hand reached down to grope her breast and squeeze so hard that she yelped. "Are you letting him touch what is mine?"

Struggling, she managed to rip free of his grasp and stumbled backwards. "I am not yours," she spat the words out like acid from her chest.

His fat face dissolved into a lethal smile as he strolled on toward her, already starting to undo the buttons on his pants. She stepped back.

"Winyo, my dear bird, has he been showing you some new tricks that has made your blood run cold for me?" he asked, "I know how to heat you up again. I will have you crying out beneath me in no time."

"Don't come any closer," she spat as she ducked from his reach.

"Winyo, Winyo, Winyo…" He drawled lazily, "Didn't you hear, he is a witch's son. Such people are not good for the family."

"No, my mother is always at their house."

"That is business. You…you belong to me," he growled low in a tone that racked through her like sharpened talons. "I don't want to see you with him, ever again. Do you understand?"

"Stay back," she hissed as she held the weeding knife between them. He halted as his gaze trailed from her to the knife then travelled to her face again - she couldn't resist the shudder of revulsion at the heat of desire as he locked gaze with her. She wanted to spit at his ugly face, anything to wipe the lust from his eyes. The smile that slit his thick lips was cold, dark and hideous.

"I remember this game," he chuckled, "I thought we were past that."

"Stay back, or– or I will hurt you."

"Stop this, Winyo!" he boomed impatiently, the sound so jolting that she nearly dropped her weapon in fright. She did drop the ground hoes but held onto the two knives.

"I–I will use this," she threatened unsteadily but she meant every word of it. There was no way that she was going to make it easy for him today. She would not help him defile her. She was no timid mouse. Guma wanted her to defend herself, and damn it, she would.

She was not going to let Uncle Saul touch her. Not today, not today-*not today*, she chanted the words in her head as tears clogged the back of her eyes.

In one swift motion that took her by surprise, he launched himself at her and was knocking one of the knives from her hands. She used the other in her left hand and slashed deep, across his belly. He howled in pain and let go.

A red haze of fury clouded her mind then, and as if on instinct, she ducked to the ground, grabbed the second knife and she was using both hands to slash at him. His howls filled her ears, sinking into her skin like the sweetest melody. She had hurt him, just like he hurt her. Finally, she was getting justice served and it felt glorious as she ducked behind him and stabbed at his back.

He attempted to wrench a knife from her but that made her wilder. She launched herself atop him and stuck her thumb into his eyes, sinking them deep into the sockets, the pained screams that followed brought a satisfied smile to her lips. She rolled away, took hold of the knife again and fervently brought the knife down to his flesh until he moved no longer.

When she finally dropped the knife, she was panting, crying, screaming and laughing at the same time. Her dress felt thick and wet with blood. Uncle Saul laid on his back in a red puddle that kept on widening as the blood drained from him. His eyes were two dark holes with blood pouring out in endless streams of red. She had ripped his stomach open and parts of his gut were sewn on the dirt.

He was …dead.

Her breath caught somewhere in her throat; her heart began a fast pace again as her mind cleared. Oh lord above, what had she done? She was trembling all over again, this time with a new form of terror.

She had just killed a man. This was not supposed to happen. She had just wanted to make him hurt like she had. Not …not this.

The knife fell from her limp fingers. Her strength diminished as she crumpled to the ground in a heap of despair. A cold numbness settled over her like a chilled blanket. *How had this happened*?

He deserved to die, she told herself, the slimy son of a dog deserved to die, but that didn't ease up her conscience. She felt worse. How had this happened to her? A man had died, lord, not just any man but her uncle, her mother's brother. What was she going to tell her mother?

Winyo thought in horror as she wrapped her arms around her trembling shoulders and rocked back and forth.

Her mother would disown her. No…no, Winyo schooled her mind, she refused to be blamed for this. She was not going to be blamed for this too, she couldn't allow that…no she would not…he…he deserved this.

Then she was thinking fast, very fast. She was not going to take the blame for this. No way. Quickly she looked around. People can get killed by robbers or wild animals, Winyo thought. She just had to make it look believable.

She heaved and dragged Uncle Saul's body next to the main road. Then she went about hiding her tracks and performed the tiresome act of cleaning up the scene. She couldn't remember ever moving this fast in her life. Even then, her heart felt numb. It was almost like the first night he had assaulted her. She felt changed, fundamentally and she would never be the same again.

She was a murderer.

8

Saul, Saul...Uncle Saul... Winyo had scratched the name against the skin of her arm. She kept on writing and tracing over the name. Blood welled from the cuts, but the bite of the pain soothed the ache in her soul that threatened to rip her mind apart with re-runs of what she had done.

Something sharp, that was what she was looking for right now, a needle, a knife, anything when her mother's irritated voice reached her.

"Winyo," Ader's voice bellowed.

Winyo wrung her hands impatiently while she waited for her mother to cross the compound. She could feel the dark demons of her mind starting to take hold of her. She needed to let out that pain before it became consuming. She had been sitting with a group of men from the village who had come to help with Saul's burial arrangements. His body had been found and the story was that he had been mauled by animals. It was said that they found wild dogs eating at him. It was assumed that he had probably been set on by robbers and then the wild animals finished him off. Winyo had stopped paying attention to the rumours after that. Nobody suspected her, which was good. She didn't think they would. Just like no one had thought that Uncle Saul would do what he had done to her.

"Winyo, what are you doing now?" Ader demanded as she

approached her. Her eyes were red rimmed from hours of crying over her brother. Winyo averted her gaze.

"Nothing."

"Remember what I told you about the burial," she began, Winyo tried to recall what her mother had told her, but everything was blurry; she had been actively trying to block so much off her mind.

"I am supposed to stay here with my brothers?" Winyo asked.

"Yes, your father and I are leaving today with the other villagers," Ader said.

The body had already been taken to Agoro for burial. Her mother's family was already there; they were only waiting for the arrival of the people from this village.

"The car has just arrived to take me and your father to Agoro. I need you to stay and monitor the Odyek wedding, make sure you have got all the relatives and the correct number of people for the meet with the bride's parents," Ader rapidly instructed. "I need you to stay and supply them with whatever they need. Make sure they pay you for it. I also need you to take care of the house and your brothers. I will be back in time to finish with the last of the arrangements, but I need you to run it smoothly."

"Okay."

"Your Aunty Atang is going to be here with you, don't stay out late in the night, do not walk alone. If– if you want to go anywhere, please go with Atang." Ader was struggling with her words as she attempted to hold back a sob as no doubt the thoughts of how her brother met his death played on her mind. It didn't take long before she was sobbing into her hands again. The sight made Winyo's gut twist painfully. It was rare to see Ader in such a state. Winyo took in a deep breath and locked down any emotion as she allowed numbness to seep into her pores.

Taking hold of herself, Ader continued, "Promise me you will take care of yourself."

Winyo nodded stiffly. And after a few uncomfortable words and hugs, her mother finally left. Winyo stood at the compound as she watched them leave. Then she went into her room to search for what she needed. She found it under her pillow. A sewing needle.

She bent over her arm and scrawled the name on her arm, wincing at the pain before the choking darkness began to clear. It was a difficult task to make the name visible, but with utmost precision, the letters come out right. *Saul...Saul...* She scrawled over the name and rewrote over again and again. The more she wrote, the less the pain burned her. By the time she was done, her arm was covered with blood. But she felt blessedly healed, but she knew the feeling would not last. It never did.

She rose to her feet. She would feel good for a while. The feeling would last a while. Then she would have to cut herself again.

She grabbed a jerrycan and was on her way to the borehole. The twins met her on her way back.

"Winyo," Apio was the first to speak, "We are so sorry for what happened to your uncle."

"How are you?" Acen asked.

"I am fine."

"Are you sure?" Apio insisted.

"Of course, she is sure. Stop pushing her," her sister lectured, "We hear that they are going to hold a clan meeting to find out who really committed the act."

"They are?" Winyo asked. "Didn't they say robbers did it? Then wild animals?"

"Yes," Apio said, "Such things have never happened in our village, everyone is shocked, you know. They say you are going to use the witch doctor from another village to find out what happened."

"Uhh..." Winyo began uncertainly, "Where did you hear that

from?"

"Our mother said Latera heard your father say it at the village drinking place," Apio said.

Acen added, "We hear he was asking for the best witch doctor around. I think he might use Opali, the witch doctor from Madi Opei, they say he is the best..."

*No, no no...*Winyo thought wildly, could a witch doctor truly reveal her secret? She had heard so many tales about witch doctors and the wondrous things that they could do, from granting fertility to finding out causes of deaths. *Oh lord!*

"They say he has been known to perform wonders," Acen added, "Uhuh, but there is surely no need, I mean, everyone knows who did it, just that no one dares mention it."

"They know?" Winyo blanched, her heart tripped and then started a fast race. Surely no one knew. She had been careful. No one knew...no one had been there...

"Odyek," the twins chorused, nodding their heads.

Odyek family? What? Winyo thought in alarm. What in the hell had she done?

"There used to be such strange deaths in the village when they were around years ago," Apio said, "Our father told us so, it is no surprise that the first murder happens a few months after their arrival."

"Yep," her sister answered, "It is them alright. Most are guessing that it is either Alice herself who did it, but since most people haven't seen her in a while, they say it could be the other one."

"Which one?" Winyo asked slowly as dread sank to the pit of her stomach and made a dark home there.

"Guma," Apio whispered as if she were afraid her revelation would be carried by the winds and delivered to the name bearer.

"People think it is him?" Winyo croaked the words past the lump that clogged her throat. Tears stung at the back of her eyes.

"May- maybe it is not them... not him," Winyo rushed defensively. Goodness above, why Guma?

Acholla joined them then and she, too, drowned her in condolences before asking what they were talking about.

"Of course, everyone knows it is them," Acholla confirmed her dread, "but of course we have to be sure."

"It may not be them," Winyo insisted.

"Do you know someone who could have hated your uncle?" Acholla asked.

Of course, she did. "No, but the Odyeks have no motive."

"They are witches, at least Alice is," Acholla blurted. "They don't care who they hurt, and the mango rarely falls far from the tree."

"Guma is the most likely of the brothers to have done that," Apio added.

"Acholla how can you even suggest that?" Winyo protested. "All he does is draw; we were just with him last time."

"Exactly," she intoned, "Perhaps that is the reason he was getting close to you, so that he could find out more about your uncle."

"What is wrong with you?" Winyo exclaimed in disbelief. "I thought you liked him."

"Winyo, my dear friend, being nice to the son of a witch does not necessarily mean I like him," Acholla explained, "You should not be calling him your friend either."

"...I mean after what he did to your uncle, you can't be together anymore," Apio added.

"...Whatever you have going on between you two, I think you should break it off," Acen suggested, nodding her head like it was the wisest sentence that she had ever constructed.

Winyo stared at them incredulously. "We are not together, and he did not kill my uncle. There is no proof."

"It is hard to accept this, believe me, I understand," Acholla said as she placed a comforting arm over Winyo's shoulders. "I suggest that you don't even talk to him, he will take the hint and back off, if he has any shred of decency."

Then the twins were giving their own suggestions of what she should do. Winyo was only glad to return safely back home. Her head was buzzing. Several thoughts running through her mind so fast that she felt the start of a headache at her temples.

Guma, good lord what had she done?

"Winyo?!" Atang was calling. Crossed, Winyo went out of the kitchen to see what the woman wanted.

She stood at the compound tying a head cloth to her hair; she was no doubt going somewhere. It was laughable that her mother had left her under this woman's care. Atang was rarely at home. Winyo hadn't discovered where she spent most of her evening but at this point, she did not care.

"What?" Winyo demanded.

"Oketch's wife came by; she said she needed some millet for her supper. I told her to wait for you but she had to start her cooking, so she left. I need you to take it to her."

Winyo glanced at the sky; it was already evening and the sun was setting fast. Oketch's hut was very far away. "Why didn't you sell it to her when she was here?" Winyo asked irritably.

"Do not get that tone of voice with me," Atang retorted. "It is your job, anyway, I don't know the prices you sell the flour for. I am not going to be accused by your mother of mishandling her items."

Winyo rolled her eyes. She didn't want to make a delivery right now, but she decided a bicycle ride would do well for her mind. Winyo clambered onto the bicycle and was soon peddling away as fast as she could to Oketch's house.

Perhaps it was the fast pace at which she was riding that caused the bicycle chain to break, she couldn't tell, but somehow the chain broke on her way back from making the delivery. She had to walk the bicycle.

She was close to home when she met Okeny, her brother's friend. Winyo sighed wearily as she recognized him in the semi darkness.

"What are you doing all alone at this hour?" he demanded as soon as she was close enough.

"Where are you coming from?" Winyo asked absently as she kept up her pace. It was obvious he had been hunting. There were some game animals in the wild and occasionally when the price of meat in the market got too high, the men in her village went to hunt. Okeny held an arrow and the spears peeped from the sack on his back.

"Hunting," he replied, "Was unlucky though, didn't catch anything, perhaps my luck just changed."

Winyo shook her head. She didn't have time to decode all his innuendos; she was already tired and she had a headache. She attempted to walk around him. He blocked her path.

Her eyes shot up to him in alarm. "Get out of my way, Okeny."

"Why?" He drawled lazily as he stepped closer, "I, too, want to get some of what you give freely to others…"

She shook her head as anger heated up her blood. She was so fed up with men trying to take advantage of her as soon as she was by herself.

"Okeny…stop."

"Richard and Okot have been talking…" His smile was an attempt at seduction that had her shaking with rage. "They sing tales of how delicious you taste, how sweetly you moan when–"

"That's enough, Okeny!" she snapped furiously. "Get out of my way."

"Perhaps I can make you moan too. You know how long I have wanted you for. Imagine my surprise when I find out that you were very friendly with Ronald and Okot…hhmm," he hummed in approval. "Took two of them at the same time. I never took you for the naughty kind, but I am not complaining."

She stepped back as cold fear and revulsion wrapped her in its familiar, cold embrace. This crap was not happening again. "Okeny, you don't want this."

He chuckled, "If you think that, then I really need to work on my communication skills."

Then he was reaching out for her. Red fury clouded her vision and all she could think of was, *oh no…he was going to have to die too.*

9

GUMA

There was only one female he wanted and she was as elusive as the wind. One minute she was warm and receptive, then the next, she withdrew from him like night from day. The most irritating part of it was that he couldn't bring himself to stop thinking about her. She invaded his thoughts every day and he dreamt about her all night like a lovesick puppy. He woke up every morning feeling more frustrated and his body raging with unfilled need for her.

She was beautiful, but not in an in-your-face kind of way, it was subtle and enhanced by her unintentional sensuality. The fact that she didn't recognize her drugging appeal only made him desire her more. He also knew that she was damaged. She was still hurting, and it scoured him that she would not let him help her. He had thought he had made some progress with her after the drawing lesson and helping her with her chores in the field, but then she had withdrawn again. Granted her uncle had just passed away, it surely was one of the reasons she would seek to be left alone, but it bothered him that she did not seek him at all, in the least, for comfort, a shoulder to cry on.

He did not know why he felt the need to be there for her, do nice things for her. There was just something about her that drew her to him like a magnet.

He was in his bedroom, drawing yet another picture of her. She truly had the most amazing brown eyes, he thought fondly as he sketched the familiar lines of her face. She always had her thick curly hair loose around her neck. Longingly, he traced the gentle lines of her chin on the drawing he held on his lap. Her face was slightly cheeky for someone so slender, but it only intensified her rare beauty.

Her skin was soft and smooth as the coconut scent that always lingered on her skin. Her lashes were long and curved, perfectly framing her large doe brown eyes, her nose was small and round. It was her best feature. Her lips were perfect, full and inviting, holding the rich vibrant coloring of the evening sunset. He loved the taste of those lips too. He recalled the heat of devouring that soft giving mouth, the soft moans from her lips as he had pressed her plush body to him...bloody hell!! Guma groaned in frustration as he fell back on the bed. He really was hopeless. He had to see her soon before he lost his damn mind.

Once he made his last pencil stroke, he balled up the drawing and tossed it to the bin. It was not perfect and she was perfect. Perhaps, he should really consider making a painting, he decided. She would look good in a painting.

"For how long are you going to just stare into the air?" Earnest asked as he strolled into the room. He fished into the bin and unfolded the piece of paper.

"Winyo," his brother laughed, "Why don't you just tell the girl that you like her so that she can reject you and you can go on being my stupid brother and making paintings that we can actually sell?"

"You are not as funny as you think," Guma snorted. Ernest only laughed harder. His brother was right though. He was the only reason that his family were still in this village. He had told them that he needed the time and isolation to create several paintings. He hadn't yet completed the third painting. It was unlike him. Well...he was distracted.

At this rate maybe his studio in Kampala was a much better work place than the tranquil savannah of this village. He earned well from his paintings even though he was only in his second year of Art Study at Makerere University in the City. His paintings were in several galleries. He had held several successful solo exhibitions in the City and had been invited a number of times to attend exhibitions in France, India, Germany and the list was endless. His most recent exhibition was to be in Kenya but... he wasn't even close to being ready considering most of his drawings were of a certain village girl with soulful eyes. He wondered if he could turn it into a single subject exhibition. Those didn't make enough money, but heck! He didn't have any other inspiration at the moment. It was like he had tunnel vision when it came to her.

Earnest was right, he had to snap out of it.

"Talk to her," his brother pressured now.

"And tell her what exactly?" he asked in frustration. "I think I have made my intentions quite obvious to her."

"Just tell her that she is wasting your precious artistic mind thinking about her," Paul joined them. "Then ask her to sleep with you, so that you can screw her out of your system and you can start functioning like a normal person again."

"...and you wonder why girls avoid you like the plague," Guma scoffed.

"She is coming over today," Paul spoke to Guma and immediately his heart lurched so hard he thought he would black out from the rush.

"Winyo is coming here?" He couldn't hide the excited grin that tugged at the corner of his lips. His brothers rolled their eyes. Earnest threw a pillow at his face. "You better talk to her today. Have her put you out of your misery."

"I will talk to her."

And he tried. Winyo showed up with a dead expression on her face. She did the right things, said the right things but she was not there. Guma had attempted to speak to her alone, but she had politely brushed him off and any questioning on how she was doing was met with cool short replies that held no room for further discussions.

By the time she left, Guma was so agitated that he nearly followed her home. But he restrained himself, blaming it on the death of her uncle. Death was hard to process, especially the death of a loved one. He knew that kind of pain. His father had only recently passed away and both he and his family were still trying to deal with the loss.

He wanted to comfort her, but she wouldn't let him. The next few days that she helped with the wedding, he felt he had lost her even more. He could feel her slipping away from him and it broke him more than he cared to admit. It seemed that the harder he tried to get to her the more distant she became. And the more he…missed her.

She came less often to his home after her mother had returned from the burial and had taken over the wedding arrangements. Unlike a church wedding where everyone shows up in church and the couple gets married and later a celebration is held at home, a traditional wedding involved a whole lot more. First, the groom had to gather his relatives and friends and have a discussion on what should be paid for the bridal price and discuss what each relative was willing to contribute. That would have been an easy part if the Odyek family had a lot of close relatives in the village, but unfortunately none of their relatives had any close ties with them and the few that did wanted nothing to do with them. Guma had never cared to find out why and the rumours that they were witch doctors was mostly annoying.

Lucky for them, they had Ader. Winyo's formidable mother. He loathed the woman for her treatment of her only daughter, but she was good with people. She somehow managed to entice and draw people into their much-avoided home. Ader got the word round that there was free brew at the Odyek house and slowly drew more of their reluctant relatives. Winyo was always ready with the local *Kwete* brew which the villagers loved so much.

Of course, the drinking only made the bridal wealth discussions last longer, also unfortunately most of their relatives wanted some sort of payment for their attendance at the wedding.

Ader had informed them that payment made to relatives was not according to tradition; in fact, it was unacceptable. But she had rushed on to explain what a shame it would be if the groom showed up to the bridal home without relatives, and the bride's family would most likely reject the groom. No one wanted that. Alice was not happy with this but just wanted the wedding to be over with.

A date had already been set for Opete's wedding. Thankfully, the wedding arrangements were nearly done. The hardest part to it was gathering a large enough entourage to support the groom. Ader had efficiently made this possible.

A few relatives were present today, but they wouldn't be staying for long, so Winyo had a lot more free time. Today Guma had decided that he would not take no for an answer. He had eagerly waited at the window, watching for Winyo's arrival. He didn't bother to resist the grin that always took over his face at the sight of her. She appeared bored, trailing docilely beside her mother who was chattering a mile per minute.

He slid off the chair at the window and made for the door. They had just got to the door when he flung it open. For a flash of a second her face lit up as if in pleasure before she shut down again.

"How are you, Guma? Is everyone in?" Ader asked.

"Yes, Mother is waiting for you," He stepped aside to allow Ader in and then blocked the door after Ader had passed through.

Winyo's eyes flew up to him in surprise, and at once he was lost in the brown depth of them.

"Am I not allowed to come in?" Winyo asked.

"No, not today," he replied smoothly.

She looked confused as she shuffled restlessly from one foot to the other. "Okay...am I allowed to ask why?"

"I have other plans for you. Plans that do not involve sitting in a room talking the same old boring stuff, that we have been doing for days."

"Those boring things are what brings us here," she stated.

"Only those boring things? Here I was thinking that you come here for my riveting conversations and irresistible personality."

Winyo laughed then. "Your modesty is admirable."

"Always," he said, reveling in the sound of her laughter. "Come with me."

She cocked a brow at him. "Where will you take me?"

He didn't have a particular place in mind, but he knew he needed a few hours alone with her. It was all he had been trying to do for days. Instead, he said, "Where is the surprise in that if I tell you? It is not like I am going to murder you or something."

She visibly tensed. "What?"

The tremor in her voice had him regretting his choice of words. He was a jerk. He wanted to flay himself for the insensitive comment. She had just lost an uncle to murder and here he was handing out jokes like he was a standup comedian.

"I am sorry," he apologized.

She faked a laugh. "No...it is nothing– it's okay."

It was far from okay; he knew that when he held her hands and felt the tremor in her small fingers, but she allowed him to guide her away from the house.

"Seriously, where are we going?" She broke the silence as they took to the path leading away from the house. "My mother won't be pleased."

There was nothing more to be done about the wedding, just final arrangements, the date was set. Every preparation for the wedding was already done; it was rather the over anxious groom who had everyone gathered again to go over what they had already done ten times before. Ader would be occupied for a while.

"I asked my brothers to inform her that we are off on an errand," he said in an attempt to ease up her worries. "I doubt she will notice that we are gone."

"She notices a lot of things," she grumbled.

He shoved down his disappointment at her continued gloomy expression. He did not want to force her to do anything, lord knows she followed orders like a well-trained dog, but he did not want her submission. He wanted her to *want* to be with him.

"If you are worried that you will get in trouble, I will take you back to the house. I don't want you to do anything that you don't agree to, little bird."

"You know what, I spend too much time with my mother, I am getting sick of her," she confessed and he couldn't help but laugh at her rare show of irritation towards her mother. She was always so sickeningly respectful of that rattle snake.

He squeezed at her hand and he said honestly, "I want to go for a walk, perhaps it will cure me of this craving to be near you."

"You crave to be near me?" she asked.

"More than I could ever put in words," he answered and let the heat show in his eyes as he stepped into her. "I know you have been avoiding me, and I don't know why. I am not going to ask for an explanation. I am only asking to spend some time with you. Grant me this."

She hesitantly nodded her head and he let out the breath that he had been holding. He was going to make sure that he took down those barriers that she had wedged between them.

He took her to the view of the savannah grassland plains - or rather they found themselves there, after walking about for hours talking about whatever. He was doing his best to pry her out of her shell and it had taken quite a bit of prodding but she had eventually cracked and was now laughing and chatting about her time at boarding school.

As she talked, her hands kept on drifting to the cloth that she had tied around her left arm. He had been noticing this action for the past few days. He hadn't understood why she had taken to tying the cloth to her arm. She didn't seem injured. Or was she? This obviously let his mind drift back to the time when he had found her slashing at her wrists and crying in the bushes. Never had he seen a sight so heart wrenching. He hadn't been able to sleep that entire night and he had walked over to her hut in the middle of the night and sat under her window and listened for any signs of distress from her. He had stayed there until it was near dawn before he had gone back home. He knew his actions were bit stalker-ish, but he cared too much for her to leave her alone. Lord knows everybody left her alone, that's why she was so broken.

"What happened to Okeny?" he instead asked as he propped against a tree and watched her from her position on a rock floor making braids out of blades of grass.

Her reaction was not what he expected. She went so very still and turned to him with fear pasted all over her features. He jerked up and was at her side in a few strides which seemed to surprise her.

"Did he do anything to you, again?" he gritted through clenched teeth.

She shook her head, and before his eyes, he watched the mask of politeness slam down her face as she smiled sweetly at him. "He did not do anything to me."

"He disappeared recently?" he said slowly as he studied her face,

"Nobody has seen him in a while, I was told the whole village is looking for him."

She sharply looked away.

"Winyo, why do I think his disappearance has something to do with you?" he queried softly.

"I don't know why you would think that," she said as she absently rubbed her hands over her clothed arm. She seemed worried...hurt. His chest clenched with raw emotion. Bloody hell! Why wouldn't she just open up to him?

"Take it easy, I don't really care where he is," he said gently. "Okeny could be rotting in hell for all I care. I don't particularly hold fond memories of him. Did he do something to you?"

She stood up abruptly and his heart sank when she said, "We need to get back."

He wanted to argue. He wanted to pursue this conversation and find out the cause for that haunted look in her eyes. However, he didn't want to lose whatever ground he had gained with her. So, he said, "Sure."

He wouldn't have truly known what was going on with her had it not been for the three children that came rushing at Winyo. They were three skinny girls of ages ranging between five and eight. Winyo said they were the younger sisters of her friend Acholla.

These little creatures kept jumping at her and tugging at her arm, hogging up the little time he had with her. They only made to leave when they neared the Odyek residence.

It was then that somehow along with the unending games of goodbye that they kept playing that one of them tugged down the cloth that bound Winyo's arm. Guma took a look at her arm and rage consumed him like an inferno. Okeny had done something to her. It was the only explanation.

His heart lodged somewhere in his rib cage as he beheld the angry red scratch marks on her arm… and the word…the words…

Okeny…Okeny… written over and over again.

10

Their mother had warned them on what to expect in this village, but he had not expected lying in bed with a broken arm, swollen eye and skin throbbing from a beat down by a group of village boys.

Guma had not known the village boys that had roughed him up; he knew very few people in the village. The level of superstition in this place was staggering. Guma had no idea why he had been set upon, but he guessed it had to do with a new rumour in the village. He would probably ask one of Winyo's friends for the latest village gossip about their family.

He had managed to limp his way back home but had collapsed at the door step. His alarmed mother had been hovering over him since then.

Today Earnest and Paul were at his side taking turns at cleaning his wounds with the herbs that their mother had mixed up. Their mother was skilled with herbs. Her knowledge of plants and their medicinal properties was admirable. Guma assumed this was probably one of the reasons that the villagers had termed her a witch. He knew it bothered his mother, but he also was aware of how much she loved growing and working with plants. It was one of the reasons that she owned an herbal medicine company in Kampala. From Winyo, he had discovered that people in this village assumed that they lived in

Kitgum town, the small equally backward town close to this village. They, however, lived in Kampala. The people in the City were less superstitious, and people there generally preferred herbal medicine, hence the popularity of Alice's business.

"We have to talk to the local council or the police about this," Earnest said as he dabbed a warm piece of cloth at his skin.

"No one will listen to us," Alice said glumly. "We just have to leave this place. I know what this village is like."

"We can't let them get away with this," Paul said heatedly.

"We can and we will," she replied, "We came to bury your father and we only stayed so that your brother would get some inspiration for his art, but at this point we can all agree that he needs a better work environment. We leave immediately after your uncle gets married."

"Mom, you cannot be serious," Paul burst out, "They just beat your son to near death and you will not do anything about it?'

"We are leaving– that is doing something about it," Alice said firmly. Guma heard her but for once he disagreed with her. He was not a violent person, but he wanted revenge of the violent kind. He knew what the people in this village were like, he had seen how they treated Winyo, and she lived here. For the hundredth time, he wondered if she would agree to leave this village. He would find for her a job at his mother's company. She had experience running a shop and she was extremely hard working.

He had not yet brought this proposal to Winyo or his mother, for that matter. He had thought they would have more time, but Alice became insistent that they leave immediately after the wedding. She had then instructed all of them to start packing up their belongings, even though the wedding was still a week away.

Winyo had checked on him in the afternoon before the wedding and luckily his bruises had faded by then and his body didn't ache as badly anymore. He had been tempted to ask her then, but her mother had been there and Ader wouldn't leave Winyo for even a moment.

When the wedding day finally arrived, he was more anxious than relieved. His Uncle Opete, the excited groom, woke everyone before the crack of dawn and had rushed them all into getting ready. The wedding was to be held at Penina's parents' house.

It was tradition that the groom had to go to the bride's parent's house, ask for her hand, and give the bridal wealth. If the parents were pleased, they would hand the girl over to him and the elders certified them as married and this started the three-day wedding celebration.

The Odyek family had enough bridal wealth. They had many gifts including twenty goats, five cows, twenty bags of millet, and thirty bags of rice, thanks to Ader. Winyo's very helpful mother who had insisted that they purchase all the cereals from her shop. Winyo had joked that her mother would do anything for business including selling off her own daughter.

She had laughed it off, but he had noted the underlying bitterness in her words. It was a shame because he would never trade her for anything- except in following the cultural tradition on bride price payment, which Ader would most certainly demand.

The crowd at the bride's home was large and the air was festive. The ushers that greeted them were friendly and as excited as the groom. Guma had never attended a traditional wedding before, but finally being here was indeed thrilling. Ader had gone through the entire detail of decoration at the bride's home and the effects were outstanding.

They were led into the hut where the wedding discussions between the two families had to take place. Outside the women sang wedding songs and danced. It was sometime in the late afternoon when the wedding agreements were finally made that they were allowed to eat. Guma had stepped out of the hut to get some fresh air, and that's when he had spotted her. As usual his heart began that wild, fast race it always did at the sight of her. She was stunning in the green traditional dress and she stood out like a flower in a desert.

She was among the women who were serving the drinks from calabashes to the elder men. Her pretty dress had been tailored to suit her slender form. It had thin arm straps and held into her small waist with a slight string before it bellowed out and ended in small delicate gold waves slightly below her knees. The dress had been a courtesy of his mother. Guma had known that she would have no party dress to wear; he had insisted that his mother do something about it and Alice hadn't minded at all. She had always wanted a daughter, but alas she hadn't been able to have one.

Winyo's right arm was bound with a green cloth. He eyed it suspiciously for a while as he found himself wondering if she was still doing it. Cutting herself. *Okeny...Okeny...* The memory of the name scribbled on the arm still sent chills down his spin.

This village was not a good place for her. He wondered if she would come with him when he eventually asked her. He knew for certain that his heart would break if she said no. He was certain that their continued presence in the village was becoming a risk for the safety of himself and his family. But was she truly safe here? He thought wearily as she watched Winyo effortlessly glide through the crowd as she served drinks. *Who will take care of you, little bird?*

His thoughts were put to a pause when Winyo took notice of him from a distance and graced him with one of those shy smiles that shot desire through him like a lightning bolt to his crotch. He was going to have to taste those lips again before the end of the night.

He made a face indicating his frustration at the wedding delay; she laughed and spilt the drink at the man she was serving it to. The old man let out an outburst and she was soon drowning him with apologies.

Guma grinned as he allowed himself to be dragged to where his brothers were now dancing to the tune of the age-old song 'Angelina,' a song about a man's love for his wife, and how their happiness was a source of envy. The chorus was what everyone knew and combined with drums and tambourines, the fevered dance went on for hours.

He wasn't much of a traditional dancer. The stomping of feet on the ground, shaking one's head and the attempt at wiggling proved so tedious that he had to take a break. The women who had dragged him into the dance were consumed with drawing more reluctant people into the circle that had formed.

He went in search for Winyo. He found her serving food on various plates that had been laid on before her, while some girls distributed them to the guests.

"Need any help?"

She looked up and shook her head; she looked exhausted. "You are royalty today, remember? The bride's family has to do everything to make the groom's family feel welcome."

"So?"

"I am not going to be the person that makes the groom's family serve food for themselves on the wedding day- at the bride's home."

He laughed. "Come on Winyo, it's not that big of a deal."

"Tell that to the clan."

He leaned in close. "Take a break and come dance with me?"

"You want me to dance with you?"

"You ask that like it is out of your range of possible activities today," he accused and she laughed at his dejected tone. "Come on little bird, have some fun, enjoy yourself, stop thinking about everyone except for me. You should always think of me," he added quickly, and she laughed again.

"Don't worry, my nightmares have a special reservation," she teased, as she allowed him to tug her into the throng of dancers.

He didn't even have to think about what a terrible dancer he was when she was with him. He quickly discovered that she was an incredible dancer. Watching her was mesmerizing and the single most beautiful thing that he had watched in a long time. This night was going better that he would have hoped for.

Later when they took a break for drinks he said, "You should have told me you were good at this."

She raised a pretty brow at him. "I am full of surprises, Guma?"

"Yes, you are," he said heatedly, unable to deny her the truth of the depth of his admiration. He reached over and traced his hands across her soft exquisite lips, wishing he was doing that with his mouth. Tension crackled in the space between them.

"Come sit with me," he said as he led her to an area with rest mats. He drew her to a mat shadowed by a large shrub but with a view of the festivities and dancers.

It was dark now and several fires had been lit up in the compound and the generator-powered flash bulbs illuminated the night. He sat on the ground and tugged her down so that she was sprawled on his lap. She glanced about worriedly.

"It's ok," he whispered into her ear. "We are well into the shadows. No one can see us." This seemed to make her relax. Taking it as the invitation it was, he boldly skimmed his hands down her side until he cupped her bottom and pressed her to him. He groaned low at the soft juicy flesh that fitted his palms.

"Hmm, so delicious," he rumbled into her skin as his lips traced the curve of her neck. She trembled in his arms and moaned so sweetly, the sound making him so hard it almost hurt.

Unable to deny himself any longer, he palmed the back of her neck and slammed his mouth against her in a rough, desperate kiss. Her taste exploded in his tongue with a burst of sensation that spiraled down to his very rigid length. She was so intoxicating; he couldn't get enough of her.

He rolled on top of her, as he ate hungrily at her mouth. The sounds of the festivities were a distant sound to the roaring blood that pounded in his ears. Her slender thighs parted and he pressed his hardness to her soft centre. He growled low and animalistic as he rocked against her. Was she wet down there? As eager for him as he was for her? His thoughts were fevered as his hands ran all over her body. Sliding his hands between them, he ran his fingers up her thigh, not taking his lips off her mouth as he dominated and devoured her like she was his last meal. She boldly took in his wildness and responded with eager abandon.

He growled with pleasure as his fingers rubbed between her legs and...gods, she was so wet and ready for him. She undulated towards him in a silent invitation that he could not deny. He could never deny her anything. He sank a finger inside her and damn near lost his mind at the hot tight wetness that clenched at his fingers. He tried to withdraw his finger out to gain some control over himself, but she moaned and lifted her hips again, he plunged his finger back and groaned into her mouth.

"I have to be inside you, little bird," he said hoarsely. "Will you have me?"

He thought he would lose his ever-living mind in the few seconds it took her to nod her consent. Not bothering to rid themselves of clothing other than the necessary, he quickly tore away her underwear, unzipped his pants and plunged deep inside her. Hot pleasure shot and consumed him as he sank deep into her sleek sheath. Her walls squeezed him so tightly they both groaned loudly as he sank all the way to the hilt.

Sliding his hands under her, he lifted her hips to him, then he started to pound inside her. Her screams of pleasure were swallowed by the din of the music and he powered harder into her, knowing that finally...finally he was inside her. She was here, giving herself so willingly to him and he was ravenous, he plowed into her until he felt her start to clench around him.

"Yes, that's it, little bird," he growled into her mouth. "Come for me." His words seemed to spur her because she wrapped her legs around his waist, angling him even deeper...hell! He was not going to last long. She undulated against him and in a mewling cry, she came apart in his arms as a powerful climax rocked her body. He gave one long hard thrust before he came inside her, harder than he had ever done in his life.

He rolled off her, bringing her to curl against him, both struggling to catch their breath.

"I didn't know it would ever feel this good," she said against his chest.

He chuckled. "I am glad to hear that I pleased you." He threaded his fingers with her and brought them to his lips for a kiss. It was then that he noticed that the wrap on her arm had come off, probably sometime in their frenzy. In the dim light of the lamps, he could make out the names scrawled on her arms. *Okeny...Okot...Ronald...*

The wounds looked only recently scabbed over. He froze as he pondered on the best way to go about this. He knew that he shouldn't bring it up at all, and this was the worst moment to bring up any hurtful sensitive conversation, but he just could not help himself.

"You promised me that you wouldn't hurt yourself," he began and immediately she withdrew her hand from him and extricated her body from his embrace like she had been set on fire.

"Why do you have those names written on your skin?" he insisted as he followed her to his feet as he zipped his pants.

"That is none of your business," she snapped with a spark he had not seen in her before and sent alarm through him.

"Tell me what is making you do this to yourself," he pursued. "I could help, I want to help."

"Then help me by keeping your mouth shut," she retorted, and with that, she stomped away from him and into the throng of dancing bodies. Guma took a moment to take in what the hell had just happened before he dashed into the crowd in search for her, but that minute had cost him, because he had lost her.

How had it gone wrong so fast, he thought wildly as he searched for her. One minute he was inside her having the best sex of his life, then the next she was gone. Guma was almost certain that she had left the party because he couldn't seem to find her anywhere. It was like she had vanished.

Guma kicked himself at his foolishness. Perhaps he should have led with asking her to come to Kampala with his family. She was twenty years old, so she was technically old enough to not need her parent's permission for anything. Most of the girls in the village married around this age. He really needed to stop thinking about marriage and this girl in the same train of thoughts.

But what was with the names? Guma wondered. Were they names of people who had done something to her? Who were these people? He knew Okeny...and he was missing.

11

They did not leave immediately after the wedding. Guma was so grateful for that, because he did not want to leave things the way there were with Winyo. He was still hopeful that he could convince her to come away with them.

Their car tyre had got a puncture, therefore they needed a new tyre, and none of his thick-headed brothers had thought about putting the spare tyre in the car on their way here. They had had no option but to ask their uncle to call up a favour from someone he knew in Kitgum to buy a new tyre. The tyre had arrived early this morning, but Guma had managed to convince Alice to push the trip until the next day.

Guma was rushing over to see Winyo at the shop when he noticed something amiss, starting with how the children he met on the road promptly took to their heels at the sight of him. When the twins Acen and Apio also scurried away from him, it was a confirmation that the problem (whatever it was) had to be related to him.

Some new rumor perhaps, he thought. By the time he arrived at the shop, the stares that he had been receiving from the villagers could have melted metal. Winyo was not at the shop. Her mother was there but she didn't seem too thrilled to see him either and gave no clear information on where her daughter was.

Winyo was either at home or in the fields, so he decided to seek her at home before making the long trip to the fields.

When he met Acholla on his way, she too made a dash to get away from him, but he had just about had enough and he held her back.

"What is the problem?" he demanded of her. The girl was trembling so hard under his hands he had to ease up his grip.

"Please don't hurt me."

He was confused. "What?"

"Don't hurt me–"

"Yeah, I heard you the first time," he snapped, "Why would I want to hurt you?"

She made it an objective to look everywhere else but his face; he had to shake her to snap her attention to him but unfortunately that only made her tremble even more.

"Acholla, please talk to me. I need to know why everyone is acting weird around me. You seem to know what it is about, so please tell me," he implored.

"Why did you do it?" she spoke to the road.

"Do what?"

"Don't pretend that you don't know," she accused.

"Say it out loud anyway," he pressed.

"Okot and Ronald…is it because they beat you up?"

Now he was really confused. The names sounded familiar, but he didn't know the guys who roughed him up. "What are you trying to tell me?"

"They…they are dead," she stuttered.

He shook his head. "What?" When she continued staring at him, it finally dawned on him. "You think I …I m-murdered them?" he rasped in shock.

"They say you did it," she accused, her eyes glittering with accusation and fear.

Good lord, this was bad, so, so bad. His mother had been right. It was dangerous for them to continue living here; he hadn't considered that level of danger before.

"What? Who says I did this? Why do you think this?" he babbled in shock. She wriggled her arm and he let her go. He took a shaky step back, his mind reeling.

Acholla shifted uneasily from one foot to the next. "Well, it is unusual that people begin disappearing and then murdered right about the time that you and your family show up in the village, considering your history here…"

He kept stepping away from her in a daze. Pain constricted his chest so hard it was almost physical, he bent down to take in a gulp of air. His mind was whirling. He knew those names…where did he know them from?

Winyo, the name floated in his mind. He had seen the names scratched on Winyo's arm. She always acted like she was hiding some big secret. What the hell did Winyo know about this? Suddenly it became his singular focus to find out what she was hiding. One thing was for certain, she knew a hell lot more than she was letting on.

Briskly he strode away from Acholla who was only too eager to watch him leave. Winyo was at home; she was washing up plates and cups. She took one look at his thunderous expression and tensed.

First thing he noticed was her arm, wrapped up in cloth from wrist to arm pit, he wondered why he had not thought it odd before.

"Why are you here?" she asked.

"What is your secret?" He went straight to the point. "What are you hiding?"

He knew he was right when sheer panic took a hold of her and she attempted to flee. He gripped her arm, keeping her in place.

"Guma, please…" she began. "Not here."

She took his arm and hastily led him to her room. The last time he had been here was when they had shared their first kiss. It all seemed so long ago now. She shut the door and turned to face him.

"Okot and Ronald are dead," he began. "There is a rumour going around in the village that I killed them or my family, I am not exactly certain of the details."

"I know," she whispered, "I heard it last night. Their bodies were found. They were poisoned."

"I didn't know that," he said, "Not that anyone would care. What I would like to know is, why in gods damned earth do you have their names scrawled on your arm?"

"What?"

He strode over to her, taking her arm and whilst maintaining eye contact, he reached down and slowly unraveled the cloth tie on her arm. There it was. Etched on her arms were the dark raised names that had scarred her skin like brands, the very names of the now-dead village boys, including Okeny and her uncle's name was scribbled there too.

"Tell me what you know." He ground the words out, not sure he wanted to know the truth. She looked fearfully around the room, obviously debating on what to tell him. Guma was sure he would demand it out of her this time; he was not letting it go, like the other times that he had before. Not when he was being accused of murder.

"I had to do it," she whispered so low that he would have missed the words if he hadn't been standing close to her.

"Do what?"

She nervously licked at her lips, her eyes darting about. "They would have kept doing it, just like Uncle Saul…"

His brows furrowed in confusion. "What did Uncle Saul do?"

"He…he…did things to…me," she said hesitantly. It took a moment for Guma to catch on with her words, and fury roared in his chest like a wild beast. He wanted to grab her uncle and make him die ten times over.

"He defiled you?" The words tasted foul in his mouth. "Why the hell didn't you tell me? Who else knows?"

"Nobody knows, they would not believe me even if I had said anything," she said in a small voice as she sank onto the ground as if drained of energy. "I did try to tell my parents that I was raped, but they thought I was lying."

Now Guma really wanted to commit murder. How the hell did her parents not believe her? His chest clogged and constricted with so much pain that he was having difficulty breathing.

"For what it's worth, I would have believed you, Winyo," he consoled, as he sank onto the ground in shock. Then a dark thought crossed his mind. He tried not to process it, but he couldn't help the question that spilled out of his mouth. "What exactly killed your uncle, Winyo?"

She flinched, and he didn't need to hear her next words to know that what he feared was true.

"I killed him," she confessed.

12

"I killed him." The words clang in his ears in endless echoes. How had it all come to this? He had known she was hiding a lot, but this was a huge pile of elephant dung that he had just buried himself in. His heart banged painfully against his chest as he traced the names on her arm.

She had killed someone. His little bird had killed someone. A person who deserved it no doubt, but he couldn't get a handle on how he felt about it. Did he want her to get away with it? Should he take the blame? He wouldn't be in this village for long to either confirm or deny it. Guma shook his head hard. This was all too confusing. He had wanted to take her with him, did he still want that?

"He– deserved it, he did...things to me," she said brokenly, her eyes pleading with his for understanding. Lord knew he understood her. He just didn't have the words to say to her. How does one respond to a confession of murder? There was no rule book or standard response. This was too much; he ran his hands through his hair in frustration.

"Winyo..." he started as he stared into her angelic sweet face. "How did you even do it?"

"With my weeding knife," she explained. "I fought him...you said I had to be strong, that I should defend myself, so I did."

"Yes, I said defend, not kill someone." This was all so messed up.

"I know, but that's what ended up happening," she wailed. "I didn't set out to do it. I wasn't even looking for him. He found me and he tried to …to assault me, again. I didn't want it. I had had enough."

Guma felt wretchedly torn. He didn't know if he should take her in his arms and comfort her like he wanted to, or just get out and run, never to see her again. The thoughts warred in his mind, twisting his gut and tearing at him like locusts. The sight of the tears that were tracking down her trembling cheeks floored him.

"Now I can't sleep, I have nightmares, it hurts, and I hate it so much. The bastard is dead, but he still manages to hurt me," she sniffed. "Writing their names on my arm helps calm me down when I get into a panic, and the pain lessens for bit."

"Their…names?" He caught on to the word and his churning mind whirled faster as he drew the connections. "The village boys…did they die by your hands too?"

She nodded slowly. "I had to…"

He wearily rubbed at his temple, unable to believe the blasted turns that this conversation was taking. "What the hell do you mean you had to?"

"They raped me."

He stared at her in shocked silence.

"You don't believe me." She threw up her hands in agitation. "Nobody ever believes me."

"Did they really?" he said through gritted teeth. She had been going through all this and he hadn't known. All this had happened? This whole damn time?

"Yes, they did. Okot and Ronald were together when they did, I didn't want them to do it again, so I made sure that they couldn't. I searched them out at the village and then I took them to the bush and fed them poisonous mushrooms. They didn't even question it. Those arrogant bastards were so excited to see me and thought I had gone to them for sex."

Guma stared at her in silence for a moment, those big tear rimmed eyes that pleaded with him. She clearly was traumatized, for multiple reasons. How did one individual shoulder all this pain? He was weighed down like a rock, and none of this had happened to him.

"As for Okeny, it was self defence. He came upon me on my way home in the evening. I had to…"

Unable to resist it anymore, he took her in his arms and held her tight. Emotion clogged up his chest as he cradled her. How the heck had she not shared this with anyone? In the long stretch of silence, she asked, "A-are you going to tell…them?"

Was he going to tell the village? That *his* Winyo was a murderer? There was no telling what those close-minded, backward people would do. He didn't know if he wanted this information to wander past this room. After all that she had already been through? Was she justified? He was way too overwhelmed to think straight. Instead, he said, "They think I did it."

"No," she said determinedly, "I won't let them blame you. I– deserve whatever they will do to me. You- you should tell them the truth. I did it, we – we will tell them together."

"Are you out of your damn mind?" he snapped, not wanting to think about what they could do to her. She had already been beaten in front of the village for having two boys fight over her (as if that was a crime). He did not have any clear thoughts as of that moment, but one thing he was certain of was that he did not want to see her get hurt. She had clearly been through hell and back.

"Nobody should find out," he said and saw the perplexion in her face. He couldn't believe he was saying those words either, but he knew in his heart that he wouldn't live with himself if he gave her out.

"Are you out of your mind?" It was her turn to ask. "I cannot let you take the blame for what I did."

"Yes, you can."

"No!" she yelled, vigorously shaking her head. He took her face into his hands and brought her to him. "We don't need to tell anyone anything. My family and I are leaving soon. No one will know."

"You are leaving?" she whispered. "Please don't leave me. I couldn't bear it; you are the only one who has kept me sane these past few days."

He rested his forehead against hers before he lowered his mouth to hers, a shudder traveling through him as he inhaled her scent. Desire racked him like feline claws as he parted her mouth and deepened the kiss. It felt natural, like something that he just had to do. He needed to taste her, just one more time. To ease both her pain and the ache for all that she had been through and for all that he had not been able to do for her. He poured all that emotion in the kiss as his tongue tangled with hers in a wicked, erotic dance. Her taste was a drug to his fevered mind. He wanted to lay her on the mattress and sink his aching shaft into her, but he held back. Again, not certain at how to act after being given such horrific news.

Slowly, he dragged his mouth away from her. "Maybe we have to stop," he said hoarsely, knowing that if she put up an argument, he wouldn't be able to resist her.

"No, we don't have to stop," she replied, denying his request as she followed his lips and returned his kiss. Blood drained from his brain and straight to his throbbing shaft. His hands trailed down the delicious soft curves of her body, exploring her. Abruptly, she rose up and he watched in awe as she untied the sash to her dress and dropped her dress, exposing soft curves that he ached to explore. She wriggled out of her panties, then crawled onto his lap like a cat, unzipping his pants.

He grew impossibly hard as she stroked him with her cool hands once, twice before she impaled herself upon him in one swift motion. He groaned long and loud as her wet sheath fisted his raging shaft. He hissed as she began to ride him hard, and he let her take control. Understanding that she needed this dominance while connecting at this basic, primal level.

He growled as she started slamming herself even harder on his stiff shaft. He filled his hands with her breasts, wanting to feel the round firm mounds bouncing in his hands, she really did have phenomenal breasts. He pinched her nipples and her head fell back in pleasure.

His gut clenched when she made a distinctive little moan; her sheath warmed, tightened around him. She was close, so close. He gripped her hair with one hand, his other hand bit into her waist as he held her still and wildly punched hips into her. Her eyes widened, her breath caught, and she tightened around him. He used his grip on her hair to keep her head up so he could watch her orgasm take her, so he could see as her eyes went blind with pleasure, her lips parted, and her brows furrowed like the pleasure was so good it hurt. Then he followed her, and he came so hard he nearly blacked out.

The sun was setting when they decided to make their way back to the Odyek residence. Winyo had insisted on accompanying him to the main road at least. She was reluctant to see him go and he almost told he that he wanted her to come with them. There was clearly nothing for her here; however, in light of all that she had revealed to him this evening, he was hesitant to be quick on that invitation. He needed to sleep over this, or maybe discuss it with one of his brothers. He wasn't sure, it was all too confusing. At the moment, he could not think straight especially with the taste of her still in his mouth and the feel of her soft body still echoing in his body like a drum beat.

They both noticed the black plume of smoke at the same time. It was blowing from the location of his home. They glanced at each other and in that instant communicated more loudly and clearly than words ever could, they broke off into a run.

Several thoughts reeling through his mind...*was the house on fire? Was his family still here? Had the villagers harmed them?* Worse yet, *were they in the fire?*

Their feet pounded hard at the dusty ground as they raced. They hadn't reached anywhere near home when his family car came to a screeching halt beside them. His brother Okwera was driving.

Earnest opened the door and roared, "Get in!"

Without thinking, Guma grabbed Winyo's arm and yanked her into the car with him.

"What is going on?" he demanded.

"The villagers think we are responsible for certain deaths in the village," his mother explained. Guma looked at the back to find that all his siblings were in the car.

"They intend to kill us in retaliation. They are burning up our house."

"What!" Guma shook his head hard to clear his mind. The sex had put him in such a state of drugged up bliss that he had forgotten all about the village gossip. He glanced at Winyo who was wide eyed beside him, and he subtly shook his head when she looked like she was about to say something. They were burning down their house, what would they do to her?

They had barely driven five meters before they were swamped by a mob of angry villagers with machetes and sticks.

"Keep driving," Alice gritted out. "They will kill us."

Okwera floored the accelerator. The crowd screamed in outrage and made to run at their car but parted to let them through. Instead, they threw spears and stones and sticks at the car, glass shattering. A stone caught Guma on the head, blood spurted through his nose and lip; he barely managed to push Winyo away from him.

Everything then happened so fast. A car came speeding from behind them, then gun shots erupted.

"They have guns?!!" Ernest shouted in anger.

"Okwera, please," Alice screamed, "Drive as fast as you can."

"I am!" he yelled back as the car swerved to the side and rammed their vehicle. Okwera struggled to keep control of the car and kept on going.

They opened gunfire again. The sound deafening as they again ducked to the floor of the car. Guma yelled as pain lanced through his left arm. One of the bullets had caught him. Then he heard Winyo scream and he nearly lost his mind.

"Winyo?!!" he demanded, but she only kept screaming. He tried to get to her, but the car was moving so fast and wildly they kept on getting thrown from one side of the car to the other.

The attacking vehicle eventually slowed and stopped. They all lay on the car floor in a daze for what seemed like centuries as Okwera sped their car away from the cursed village.

"What happened? Why did they stop?" he heard someone ask.

"They probably ran out of gas," Alice said. "Is everyone alright?!"

Almost everyone had gotten some sort of injury or bullet wound, but it was Winyo who lay nearly limp at the floor of the car.

Guma gritted his teeth against the pain on his arm as he knelt beside her. There was a gaping hole in her middle that leaked blood profusely. She tried to open her mouth to speak but coughed up blood in litres. Panic like none other took hold of him. She could not die, she could not!

"Mom!" Guma demanded, "Do something."

"We have to stop the bleeding until we get her to a hospital," Alice said as she knelt beside him and pressed wads of cloth to her chest. "Hopefully, she can make it."

She did make it. They had arrived at Kitgum Hospital and she had been taken to surgery immediately. Guma had made sure that his was the first face that she saw when she opened her eyes.

A ghost of a smile had lifted the corner of her lips as her eyes spoke to him. Guma stared into her eyes, those expressive brown eyes and made a vow that he had every intention of keeping.

"Never again will I let any of those people get to you, little bird," he promised as he kissed her hand. "Never again will you feel unsafe."

A tear had rolled down her eyes and she gave him a slight nod and joked, "My mother will be pissed."